**"This is quite the** filled the house, brighter than it l

"Many babies' first beds are bureau drawers." Truth be told Hank hadn't gotten the cradle made before his death, but Cora didn't want to talk about that. The happiness Luke brought with him made the air inside fresher than a spring breeze outside.

Luke stroked Henry's cheek with his knuckle then turned shining eyes to Cora. "I'd hoped he'd be awake to see if he had his ma's pretty green eyes."

Again, Cora's cheeks flamed. This time she turned from Luke's gaze. "It's too soon to tell, I think." She stuffed her hands in her apron pockets, worrying the fringed inner seam.

Heavy footfalls sounded behind her, and she turned to find Luke moving toward her. "Let me check the wood box for you. I can fill it while I'm here. We wouldn't want Henry catching a chill."

"That isn't necessary, Luke. Besides, you're in your fancy suit."

"My work clothes are here." Luke looked around their cozy home. "Somewhere."

*This is no way to run a business,* Cora chided herself.

**Books by Rose Ross Zediker**

Love Inspired Heartsong Presents

*Wedding on the Rocks*
*The Widow's Suitor*

## ROSE ROSS ZEDIKER

lives in rural Elk Point, South Dakota, with her husband of twenty-eight years. Their grown son has started a family of his own. Rose works full-time for an investment firm and writes during the evening or weekends. Some of her pastimes include reading, sewing, embroidery, quilting and spoiling her granddaughters.

Besides writing inspirational romance novels, Rose has many publishing credits in the Christian children's genre. She is a member of American Christian Fiction Writers. Visit Rose on the web at www.roserosszediker.blogspot.com.

# ROSE ROSS ZEDIKER

# The Widow's Suitor

♡

HEARTSONG
PRESENTS

Recycling programs
for this product may
not exist in your area.

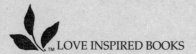 LOVE INSPIRED BOOKS

ISBN-13: 978-0-373-48696-0

THE WIDOW'S SUITOR

Copyright © 2014 by Rose Ross Zediker

www.Harlequin.com

**Printed in U.S.A.**

Do not be yoked together with unbelievers.
—*2 Corinthians* 6:14

With love to my spunky granddaughter,
Brooklyn Mya Zediker.

# Chapter 1

An intense pain snaked around Cora Anderson's bulging middle, squeezing out her breath. She grasped a straight-back chair for support. Bending into the pain, her white-knuckled grip shook the chair until a snap crackled through the room. The once-sturdy back slat wiggled loose in its groove under the pressure of her hold.

The baby was due in April, not March. Her labor pains came on fast and hard. She tamped her scream down to a throaty whimper. Gradually, the pain subsided to mild discomfort. She'd have only a few minutes before the next round of labor began.

Cora bowed her head, knowing full well one should come before the Lord on bent knee, but under the circumstances she hoped the Lord would forgive her this one transgression.

"Most merciful Father, help me bear the pain of childbirth. Please get Bertha home before the baby comes. Amen."

Bertha should have returned from delivering the railroad men's laundry before lunch. It was half-past noon. Cora knew her mother-in-law often took the long way home, making a stop at Hank's grave on the other side of the homestead. Their loved one's death had changed Bertha, made her bitter. Yet, despite Bertha's ill-tempered disposition, Cora had never wanted to see her mother-in-law as badly as she did at this moment.

The cookstove began to remove the chill from the one-room house. At the first sign of labor, she'd stoked it well so that when the baby came it wouldn't catch a chill. Cora fanned her face with her hand. Although she'd prefer opening a window to let the cool spring air in, she had to think of her little one's needs.

She lifted her seamless one-piece apron and used the edge to wipe her sweat-dampened face. Where was the bucket? She'd been on her way to fetch water to boil when she'd almost succumbed to the last pain. The bucket lay on its side by the stone fireplace Hank had lovingly built in their home.

The familiar sorrow embedded in her heart intensified. They'd planned to spend the winter evenings in front of a roaring fire. But then Hank took sick and didn't live to see the first log lit.

"Lord, be with me." Cora whispered her plea between breaths.

Most days the house seemed small and cozy, and so much better than the sod shack they'd lived in their first four years homesteading. It was just one square room with a loft built in the corner for Bertha's bedroom. Today, the pain made the room seem double in size.

The faint clip-clop of horse's hooves sounded outside the house.

Bertha was home! Hope lifted her heart and relief flooded her aching body. She regained control of her normal breathing pattern and took a tentative step toward the bucket. Her shaking legs protested. Two steps away from it, a knock rattled the wooden door, echoing through the stillness of the large open room.

Why was Bertha knocking?

The door vibrated harder with the firm rapping. "Hello." A male voice called through the door.

A niggling of pain weakened her already trembling legs. She had to get to the door before the hurt spread through her body.

Taking short, quick steps, she tried to race the impending pressure of the next labor pain. She reached the door. Gripping its frame, a white-hot cramp seized her body, kneading the air from her, much as she worked the weekly bread dough.

*Push, push, push.* She fought the natural urge.

Cora leaned her shoulder against the doorframe. She gritted her teeth until her jaw twitched, trying to keep the sound of her pain inside. Her hand tremored with weariness, which made it difficult to twist the glass doorknob. After two attempts, the door sprang open.

A young man in a dandy suit held a pillowcase in his left hand. His brown eyes widened as he searched her face.

Not Bertha. A customer.

She greedily sucked in air.

"Are you Cora Anderson?"

She nodded. The simple movement jarred her tormented body. Dare she unclench her jaw? Would she be able to speak or would the pain scream from her? She wrapped her right arm around her belly, the worn cotton calico fabric of her dress wet with perspiration, dampened her apron front.

Confusion settled on the handsome stranger's face. He smoothed two fingers over his coal-colored moustache. She had to try to talk, be polite. She couldn't turn a customer away. She and Bertha needed to take in more washing and ironing if they wanted to stay in their home, prove up their western South Dakota land. She wasn't going to let Hank's hard work go to waste. Bertha and this baby were the only family she had left, and she planned to keep them together in this home.

"M...m...may." Agony stuttered her words. Her stomach muscles clamped hard. Convulsing pain bent her over, twisting her body into the open door. Her knees buckled. Unable to bear her own and the baby's weight, she fell forward toward the wool-clad gentleman.

For a brief moment their eyes met. Fear flitted through the stranger's dark irises before Cora succumbed to the pain. Her eyes fluttered shut.

Her body thudded against something solid. In an instant she floated through the air, wrapped in secure arms.

Had she died during childbirth? Was Jesus holding her tight on the way to Heaven?

Her body relaxed at the thought of her Savior and the certain reunion with her beloved Hank.

"Hank." She stopped floating when she called his name, coming to rest on something soft and comforting.

"No, ma'am, the name's Luke."

The deep male voice cut through her fog-filled mind.

"Saint Luke?"

"No, ma'am. No one's ever thought I was a saint. My name is Luke Dow."

His voice sounded muffled, distant. Darkness threatened her consciousness. In her weak state she tried to fight against it. The pain enveloped her, fogged her mind.

The sharp clang of iron meeting iron disturbed her dreams.

Cora opened her eyes. Bright sunlight filtered through the wide-open door, illuminating the rough rafters of the ceiling. She ran her hands over the knobby string knots of the tied quilt on her bed. She hadn't died.

A shadow filled the entry. "I'm putting a kettle on to boil."

The man, Luke, shoved the door shut with his foot. The motion, combined with the heavy bucket, threw off his balance. His bowler hat slid askew on his head, revealing dark wavy hair.

Her breath came in pants. She turned her head in the direction of the cookstove. Luke poured water from the bucket into the kettle she'd placed on the stovetop.

He turned, centering himself between the kitchen and the bed. His brown eyes swam with concern. "Is someone coming to help you?" His gaze dropped. He twisted the toe of his boot. Eyes still downcast, he gave his head a small jerk. "I think it's almost your time."

Shame burned through Cora with the awareness of her soaked skirt. Another splitting pain roiled through her and she called out for Bertha. She clamped her teeth together. Nodding quickly, she turned her face away from the stranger who was seeing her in this intimate condition.

All of her muscles tightened. She closed her eyes, forcing tears out of the corners to trickle down her cheeks.

Push, her muscles commanded her body. She fought the urge. The pressure within her gained strength, ripping through her body, cutting her in two. Torrents of pain sucked at her consciousness.

Luke hovered over her. Concern etched his features,

confirming her fear. This wasn't normal. Something was wrong. She was dying.

Shame forgotten, she reached out a hand to him. His large hand engulfed hers. A scream echoed through the room. With all her might, she squeezed his rough flesh. Anything to hold her soul in this world until Bertha arrived home. She wanted to die in the arms of a loved one, as Hank had died in hers.

Cora waited for this round of labor to run its course, become a quiver of discomfort. Instead, another wave of cramping began. Every muscle in her body followed the pain's command, squeezing and pushing down to rid her body of its discomfort.

She closed her eyes. The pain increased, her pounding pulse dulled her hearing. Somewhere from far away, she heard someone call out, "What have you done to Cora?" before giving up her fight, and letting the torrents of pain wash her into a black abyss.


"What have you done to Cora?" A stout woman banged through the door. The heaviness of her footsteps beat out her anger on the rough-hewn floorboards.

Luke dropped Cora's fragile hand like it was a hot branding iron searing his palm and jumped from the edge of the bed where he sat, hoping to be a comfort to the poor girl. Muscles limp, her hand thumped on the feather mattress.

"Nothing." Luke despised the defensive whine in his voice. He'd done nothing wrong. The older woman should thank him for staying and caring for the distressed young woman. "She collapsed in my arms. I think it's her time."

Using all of her girth, the woman pushed her calico-clad body between him and the bed.

"It's not proper, a stranger seeing a woman this way."

She quickly pulled a worn quilt from the end of the bed, covering Cora's water-stained skirt.

She turned to face Luke. The stiff ruffle of her wool bonnet brushed his moustache and the tip of his nose when she tilted her head to look him in the eye. Her narrowed-eyed stare and stern expression reminded him of a prairie rattler prepared to strike. He stepped backward. Once adequate space separated them, he met the lady's icy stare.

Sturdy arms folded in front of her, she broke eye contact. She looked him up and down. "I know all the people in the area, because there aren't very many. Who are you?"

"Luke Dow. I came to..." His eyes darted to the doorway. The long-forgotten pillowcase holding his dirty clothes lay lifeless and limp on the porch, similar to the sweet young woman on the bed. What did it matter why he was here? A person would think the woman would be happy someone stayed with her daughter, who seemed to be badly in need of attention, unless...

Dread shivered through him. He nodded his head toward the bed. "Is she dead?"

The older woman, who must be Bertha, cocked her head toward the bed. "She's breathing." A deep sigh heaved her chest. "What should be a joy has turned into a burden."

Her puckered mouth made her look like she'd swallowed a spoonful of powdered alum.

The curtness of her statement and her expression raised Luke's hackles. From what he could tell once he entered their home, the young woman, even in intense pain, had tried to prepare for the arrival of the baby. Triangular white flannel lay on the table beside a tiny nightgown and a pastel quilt. The fire in the cookstove had been stoked, and by the placement of the water bucket, her labor had interrupted the chore. Had the older woman no heart, no compassion? She'd left her young daughter alone in her time of need and now, the sweet young woman lay on death's door.

"Are you Bertha?" Luke's tone lacked the respect any elder deserved.

"Yes." Bertha made no attempt at pleasantries. She pulled the strings of her bonnet, untying the bow under her chin.

"She's been asking for you." Perhaps knowing she was needed, wanted, would defuse her anger.

Bertha slipped the bonnet from her head. Her tight-plaited black hair, spun with silver strands, haloed around the crown of her head, emphasizing her stern expression. "What are you doing here?"

The combination of his wool suit, the temperature of the room and Bertha's accusing stare, beaded sweat on Luke's brow, dampening the band of his bowler where it rested on his forehead.

"I heard you take in washing." Although he wished he hadn't. Some of the railroad men had pointed him in the direction of a young widow who charged a fair price for washing and ironing clothing.

A low moan cut through the silence in the farmhouse. Luke stretched to his full height, peering over Bertha's shoulder at Cora. Sweat beaded on her ivory skin, brown ringlet wisps stuck to her damp face. Pain pinched her eyelids tight, covering her pretty eyes.

Luke kept his gaze on Cora. He guessed she was barely twenty. What a pity she'd never make it through childbirth. Couldn't Bertha see that? Or maybe she could, but she just didn't care. If he was a praying man, and he *wasn't,* he'd ask God to be merciful and take them both. A child shouldn't suffer the blame and guilt of killing his mother during childbirth.

Hurt squeezed his heart at the cold realities of the life

this child might lead. He set his jaw, dragging his gaze from the lovely young woman to Bertha's dour expression.

"You heard right. We take in washing and ironing." Walking past him, Bertha raised an eyebrow and gave a curt nod.

"I put water on the stove." A silly thing to say, but didn't women boil water for the birth of a baby?

Bertha's eyes darted to the corner of the room housing the cast-iron cookstove, verifying his statement. Why would he lie about heating water? Everything about this woman put him on guard.

She removed a white apron from a peg on the wall before hanging her bonnet over the rounded end. She efficiently slipped the apron over her head, tying the strings in a secure back bow.

After a quick survey of the kettle and wood bin, she turned to him. "Since you're here, you'll need to do the chores. Neither one of us can tend to them today. You can start by unharnessing the horse from the wagon and brushing him down."

Defensiveness gurgled in the pit of Luke's stomach. He'd taken his last command when he'd fled west. Firming his stance, he met Bertha's narrow-eyed stare, intending to set this woman straight, elder or not. No one ordered Luke Dow around. Not anymore.

He opened his mouth, but at the same time a small whimper came from behind him. He turned. His heart sagged. Pain pinched and twisted Cora's features just before a scream echoed through the small cabin.

"Get a move on. There's no call for a man to be present during childbirth." Bertha shooed one hand at Luke while pushing past him with a dipper of water. "Fill the water trough, and chop us more wood. The woodpile is by the sod house." She jerked her head toward door. "It shaped up to be a warm spring day. There's a large brimmed hat on a peg in the sod house. It belonged to my son, Hank, and will serve you better than your citified hat."

Luke stared at the woman in disbelief. Who was she to question his attire?

"Go on now." Bertha flipped her hand through the air, dismissing him from the room.

The gall of this woman thinking Luke was there to do her bidding. She was right. He needed to leave. He'd gather his laundry and go back to camp. He turned on his heel. His heavy steps thundered across the floor. Grabbing the doorknob, he threw open the door. Imagine, Luke Dow, a businessman, doing homestead chores.

He crossed the threshold. A high-pitched moan filled the room, prickling his skin, raising the hair on his neck. He stopped and glanced over his shoulder.

Bertha sat on the edge of the bed, one arm under Cora, lifting her head while putting the enamel dipper to her lips. The color had drained from Cora's face, giving her the pallor of a bleached sheet.

Luke closed the door on the sad scene, his belief in God's nonexistence reinforced. He removed his hat, raking his coarse wool jacket sleeve across his damp forehead. He hated taking orders. This one time he'd oblige, though, since death seemed to be knocking on this family's door. Replacing his hat, Luke strode toward the buckboard wagon.

A bloodcurdling shriek sent a cold shiver down Luke's spine. He glanced toward the house, knowing that had to be the last sound the young woman would ever make.

# Chapter 2

A small glow shone through the four-pane window, casting strange shadows on the plank porch. In different circumstances it would seem welcoming to Luke. Dread pulled at his heart the entire time he performed the chores. He hoped her last scream wasn't the baby's first breath. Living that life was too cruel. More than once, Luke had wondered where God was when these situations happened.

He shifted the crude leather carrier filled with wood on his shoulder, raised his hand to knock and hesitated. Steeling himself for what lay beyond the door, he closed his eyes and drew in a deep breath.

An inviting aroma filled the air. His stomach rumbled. His eyes popped open. Rubbing the bristly hair of his moustache with two fingers, he frowned. It wasn't so odd that Bertha had made dinner. A person had to take nourishment during mourning to prevent illness. Hopefully, she wasn't in such a state he'd feel obligated to stay. He'd drop the wood in the bin, express his condolences and head back to his camp.

Rapping his knuckles lightly against the whitewashed door, Luke waited for permission to enter.

The door swung open. Bertha wiped her hands on a muslin apron. "Don't stand there letting the chilly air in." She jerked her head toward the inside of the house.

Luke removed his hat, realizing he still wore the one Bertha had suggested. It was a size too big. He'd tied a handkerchief around his head to hold it in place. He pulled the white linen hanky down his face until it hung in a loop around his neck. He stepped across the threshold so Bertha could close the door, keeping his eyes downcast and his back to the bed.

"Go on, now. Put the wood away and wash up. Supper's ready."

"What?" Luke's eyes darted to the table. Two places were set with blue tin plates and flatware. His heart squeezed at the number of place settings.

"I said supper's ready. Put the wood away and wash up." Bertha's commanding tone was matter-of-fact.

"That's not necessary."

"Of course it is." Bertha placed her fisted hands on her hips. "You've put in a good day's work. I'm obligated to feed you. Besides..." Bertha hung her head. Lifting her eyes to meet his, her voice became humble. "It's the only payment I can offer."

The tightness in Luke's throat didn't allow him to respond. He worked the felt brim of the worn hat with nervous fingers, tipping his head in thanks.

Taking a side step to keep his back to the bed, Luke heard a squeak. Odd. He didn't feel the floorboard give. The noise sounded again. A mouse maybe? His eyes scanned the floor. The evening's shadows made it hard to see creatures that blended in with the wood's hues, skittering across the floor.

He needed to make this meal quick. See if Bertha had neighbors to help during this time of loss. He hurried to the wood bin and slipped the carrier off his shoulder. The wood thundered into the container.

"Shush." Bertha hissed when she walked past him to the cookstove. She scraped a long wooden spoon through something boiling in a cast-iron kettle. A promise of mouth-watering food filled the warm air of the house.

"It's all right, Bertha. It didn't wake Henry."

Luke spun around, eyes wide. Cora sat propped up in bed. An ivory crocheted shawl was draped over her shoulders. She cradled a tiny bundle in her arms.

"You're alive." His disbelief breathed out with each word.

A small smile lifted her rosy pink lips. The flickering lantern by her bedside caught the amusement in her eyes. "Yes, we both are." She tilted the bundle.

The top of a small head, with dark wispy hair, stuck out of the quilt.

"Come closer and take a good look at my strapping boy." Cora's features softened when she dropped her eyes to the quilt. Her hand caressed the top of the baby's head. Luke's heart swelled. She looked delighted with her child.

He took a step closer. The brown curly hair that had clung to her sweat-soaked face earlier was now neatly brushed and secured with ivory combs. Her green eyes, no longer dulled by pain, sparkled with each flicker of the lantern flame.

"Not so fast." Bertha caught his arm with her hand. "You need to wash up first."

"Yeah, right." Luke turned, looking around the kitchen for a washbasin.

"It's through the drape. Put the hat on the peg." Bertha waved in the direction of her bonnet.

After folding a thick towel, Bertha lifted a teakettle from the back of the stove. Luke followed her past the stove and through the drapes. She lit a lantern and poured hot water into an enamel basin.

"There's water in the pitcher if you need to cool this down. Blow out the lantern when you're through." Bertha scooted around him to exit the cramped room, her skirts grazing his pant legs.

On each side of him shelving lined the wall from floor to ceiling. Various-sized canning jars and several heavy crocks filled only a quarter of the storage space. The rest of the planks sat empty, gathering dust.

The washbasin stood along the short wall of the room. The spindles and towel bars were carved in intricate spirals. A curved flat shelf rounded the back of the opening for the basin, holding the essentials needed for personal cleanliness. The steam from the hot water clouded the attached shaving mirror.

Luke ran his hand over the beautifully crafted wood that seemed designed to hold a pitcher and basin of the finest china, rather than the simple white enamel set being used by Bertha and Cora. He lifted the pitcher from the lower shelf and gently poured water into the matching basin, flicking his fingers through the liquid until it felt tepid.

He rolled up the sleeves of his shirt then splashed water on his face and arms. A thick cake of lye soap rested on a small enamel plate beside the basin. Luke worked up a frothy lather in his hands, squeezed his eyes tight, and covered his face in a series of rough scrubs. Blindly, he repeated his motions to cover each arm. Experience had taught him a hard lesson about getting lye soap in his eyes, a burning sensation he preferred never to experience again.

Once the bitter cleanser was rinsed from his body, he reached for the flour sack hanging from another round-ended peg, and patted the moisture from his face. The freshness of his skin didn't cover the soiled smell of the blue wool shirt and brown trousers he had pulled from the dirty laundry before he did the chores. He wished he hadn't left his suit in the barn.

For a brief moment he considered going out to change. The delicious scents filling the house convinced him otherwise. His stomach pleaded for food. He pushed back the burlap pantry drape.

Cora smiled at him. "Now, you can come and look." Her proud expression showed her belief that anyone would want to look at her baby. A twinkle gleamed in her eyes, the bloom on her cheeks the color of a poppy. You'd never know she'd knocked at death's door just hours earlier.

Luke waited for Bertha to carry the heavy cast-iron pot to the table before lightly walking toward the bed. He knelt on one knee.

Cora tilted the bundle forward, her fingers working the quilt away from the baby's face. "Meet Henry. Henry this is Luke."

Splotches of dark wispy hair covered a perfectly shaped head. Barely visible eyebrows arched above closed eyelids fringed with short lashes. A peanut of a nose led down to a puckered mouth.

"He has a dimple." Luke lifted a finger to touch the slight divot in the little one's ivory chin, thought better of it and pulled his finger back.

"It's okay." Cora lifted a tiny hand from the blanket. "You can touch my son. After all, you were a comfort to me in my time of need."

Heat crawled up Luke's neck and spread to his cheeks. "It was nothing."

"No." Feathery softness touched his hand, drawing it nearer to the baby. "It was kind. Thank you for your kindness."

Luke pulled the quilt away from Henry's chin, finding it hard to take his eyes off the cherub resting in his mother's arms, and understood Cora's jubilant expression. He gently traced the newborn's cheek with his knuckle, stopping at the dimple. Henry wrinkled his forehead and gave his head a quick jerk.

"Oh!" Luke pulled his hand back.

"I think you tickled him." Cora laughed.

"And he didn't care for it." Luke smiled at the boy, who was once again serene and content.

Luke marveled at the miniature features of the baby boy. Tenderness flooded through him. He reached out and traced the soft pink skin of Henry's cheek with his index finger. "Henry is a fine name."

"He's named after his father." Cora cooed in the baby's direction.

A sharp intake of breath and the rattle of enamel meeting wood interrupted their conversation.

Cora raised her eyes to Luke, then fixed her gaze on Bertha.

He turned. Bertha stooped to pick up a mug that had fallen to the floor.

"Henry, my husband whom we called Hank, took ill last September. We lost him before the first snowfall. He was Bertha's last remaining blood kin until now. God has comforted our mourning and extended Bertha's family with this wonderful little man."

The hair on the back of Luke's neck bristled. *God* and *comfort* didn't belong in the same sentence.

Bertha straightened. Her misty eyes focused on the baby. Her lips formed a sad smile. "He does favor my son." With quick steps she rounded to the opposite side of the bed and lifted the baby from Cora's arms. "It's time for Momma to eat."

Her sturdy arms rocked the bundle until she reached a wicker basket beside the cookstove where she gently laid him down.

So Bertha wasn't Cora's mother; that explained her harsh treatment of Cora.

After fumbling with the quilt, Bertha turned, the dour expression locked back into place. "Have a seat Mr. Dow."

"Please, call me Luke."

"I'm sorry." Cora held out her hand. "We haven't been rightly introduced. I'm Cora Anderson. This is my mother-in-law, Bertha Anderson."

"Luke Dow." His large hand swallowed up Cora's during their handshake, her soft touch foreign, yet pleasing. "Maybe you remember. I told you earlier."

"Weren't you wearing a suit?" Cora looked directly into his eyes.

"Yes, ma'am. Pardon me; I changed into the soiled clothes I'd brought to be washed. I didn't want to dirty my suit."

"That was very wise of you."

Bertha pushed between them. "Supper's on the table." She glared at Cora, who lowered her eyes, taking the plate of food Bertha offered.

Anger growled inside of Luke at the way Bertha treated Cora. At least she had someone to love, and be loved by. Didn't she know how lucky she was? Luke frowned at the question that had formed in his mind. He turned on his heel, stalking the few feet to the table. Why did he care? All he needed was to get his clothes washed, not to get involved with this family. Any family. He'd had more than his fill of family in twenty-three short years.

He stood by the straight-back chair until Bertha settled herself on the opposite chair. At least she'd set the table so they could see and include Cora in the mealtime conversation. Before he was seated, Bertha heaped a large scoop of thick stew on his plate. He'd eat this portion, then leave, taking his dirty laundry with him. Surely, there was another homestead wife who needed to earn a few extra coins.

He lifted his fork.

Bertha's brows and mouth puckered in unison. "We say grace at this table."

He needed to leave. Get up, walk out and never look back. His stomach pleaded for the food before him. He laid the fork back on the table.

Bertha closed her eyes. Clasping her hands, she bowed her head. Luke's eyes darted to the bed, Cora's stance mirrored Bertha's. At least the women weren't aware he showed no reverence to their God.

With the last "Amen," Luke gripped the fork and dug into the hearty stew. The spiced meat and potatoes, although flavorful, wasn't something he'd tasted before. Luke lifted a thick slice of bread from the plate that Bertha offered. He dunked it into the brown gravy.

"I've never tasted anything this delicious before." Luke smiled his appreciation to Bertha.

"It's mutton. We're sheep farmers."

"Sheep? Isn't this cattle country?" Luke balanced his fork on the edge of the blue plate.

"Yes. Hank felt there was room for both." Cora smiled at Luke, hoping he'd begin to eat again. Most people in the area loathed sheep and sheep farmers. Their neighbor Clement and many others in the area would starve before they ate a piece of mutton. "Sheep provide two sources of income—wool and meat."

Luke pursed his lips and tilted his head back and forth, weighing her words. Or perhaps choosing his carefully.

Relief surged through her when his fingers wrapped around the fork.

"Tell us, Mr. Dow, what brought you to this area? By the cut of your earlier attire it wasn't farming or ranching. Are you a railroad man?" Cora lifted a dainty bite of her stew to her lips. Her overexerted body begged for a hearty spoonful. When Luke dropped his gaze to his plate, she scooped a heaping forkful to her mouth to satisfy her rumbling stomach.

"I'm following the railroad. They purchased land to build a terminus. People will be able to claim land alongside the track's path. I plan to claim a spot and if I'm the highest bidder at the auction, I'll build a hotel."

Determination settled on Luke's features, reminiscent of Hank's when he decided to leave the comforts of the East to homestead in South Dakota.

Bertha snorted. "Who will stay there?"

Clearing his throat, Luke leaned forward. "The railroad intends to birth a town. Many new settlers and travelers will need a place to stay." The hope glowing in Luke's eyes sent a shiver of excitement through Cora. More people might mean a brisker laundry and ironing business.

"Our best wishes for your business venture. I'm sure you'll build a fine establishment," Cora interjected before Bertha could respond.

Bertha had never wanted to head west to homestead. But she didn't want to be alone, either. So, grudgingly, she'd packed her belongings and accompanied them, dampening some of their excitement.

Now Cora would keep her from stealing Luke's enthusiasm. She could tell he was a fine man by the way he stayed by her side until Bertha had arrived.

"Thank you, ma'am. Settlers have streamed into Edson, Caton, and Dunnebeck. Like nomads, we're poised to move in a few hours when the railroad announces the location of the terminus, so we can establish our chosen businesses."

"No one is going to build a town by the Cheyenne River Reservation," Bertha harrumphed.

"I don't know. It would explain the growing number of railroad men bringing us their wash. If the railroad planned to build by those other towns, the men wouldn't travel out of their way to bring their laundry to us." Cora shrugged at Bertha's pointed look.

"Well, ladies, I have it on good authority from a railroad worker the tracks will be laid about a mile south of here. The railroad offices will make their announcement anytime now. I hope it wasn't today or I'll be behind in staking a claim. I want land close to the railroad depot so my hotel is the first establishment the disembarking passengers see when they step off the train."

God had certainly blessed them today! First, sending Luke to their door at the right time, and now, he delivered wonderful news. The laundry business might double. She'd have easier access to sell wool and sheep. She'd be able to prove up their homestead.

Cora balanced her empty plate on her legs and clapped her hands together. "How wonderful. Imagine, Bertha, a town a mile away." Enthusiasm bubbled in her voice.

Bertha turned, sitting sideways on her chair. She slowly chewed a bite of bread. "Don't get too excited over a stranger's stories. I can't imagine why anyone would think the edge of reservation land was a good spot to build a town, let alone a terminus. Let's wait until later this week when Clement picks up his wash. He'll know what is really going to happen."

"Ma'am, I'm not a liar." Luke pushed back from the

table. The straight-back chair's legs scraped and bounced across the wood floor, the same way a schoolmarm's dull chalk squeaked across a blackboard.

"I didn't mean to imply you were a liar." Bertha held up a halting hand. "Clement is a trusted neighbor and Cora's suitor. The Good Book says the man is the head of the household. Cora needs to consult Clement in matters of life."

"Bertha." Cora's raised voice quieted her mother-in-law and stirred a whimper out of Henry. She glanced toward the basket; the blanket wiggled. Although it was about time for the baby's dinner, Cora hated to wake him sooner than need be.

"Mr. Dykstra is not my suitor." Aghast, Cora fought to keep her voice a firm whisper.

Bertha pursed her lips and narrowed her eyes. "He wants to be and he has my permission. Now that the baby is born, it's time you allow him courting rights."

Cora felt at a disadvantage propped up in bed, covers tucked tight around her tired, achy body. Holding her empty plate in one hand, she shifted until she sat up straight in the bed. "Mr. Dow, I'm sorry to have a confrontation in your presence."

She had seen the same flicker of concern flash through his brown eyes before she collapsed in his arms earlier in the day. His compassion touched her heart and gave her strength to continue. "Bertha, we've discussed this. I'm mourning the loss of Hank. It's not proper to consider a suitor for at least year."

"I believe we left proper back in the civilized East." Bertha huffed.

A high-pitched squeak came from the basket.

Bertha raised her eyebrows at Cora. "Someday little

Henry will need more than mother's milk to live. Clement can provide a good home."

Luke stood, raking his long fingers through his wavy hair. He stretched his neck to peek over at the wiggling quilt in the basket. The sadness that masked his face when he turned back to Cora tugged at her heart. They seldom had company and their bickering ways were driving Luke from their home.

"I'll beg your pardon, ladies. This is family business. I'll be taking my leave."

"We haven't discussed your laundry." Her words came too quickly, and although she didn't know why she felt this way, she hoped he'd stay longer.

Luke ground the toe of his boot on the wood floor. "You have your hands full, maybe I'll..."

"You change back into your dandy suit and leave your clothes on the porch. I'll gather them before bed." Bertha fisted a hand to her hip. "Your laundry will be ready by the end of the week."

Cora grimaced at Bertha's brusque treatment of Luke. Luke's moustache bounced with the pucker of his lips. He glanced over at Henry, raised an eyebrow and gave Bertha a curt nod.

"Thank you for supper." He shifted his attention to Cora. "Ma'am, I'm glad to see the bloom on your and the baby's cheeks." His lips curved into a broad smile.

Proper or not, Cora's heart pitter-pattered.

## Chapter 3

Cora returned the heavy iron to the flat top of the hot cookstove when she heard a commotion outside the door of their house. Rubbing her sore lower back, she crossed the room to the open bureau drawer to check on Henry. The peaceful face of her sleeping child brought a smile to her lips and fortified her resolve to keep a roof over their heads by proving up their homestead.

The day he was born, the future began to look brighter. If Luke was right about the railroad building a terminus, they were sure to take in more washing and ironing, and have a way to take their sheep to market.

She caressed Henry softly, sending a quiver through him. The quilt rustled with his movement. Turning, she walked to the south window. Her body still ached from the effects of Henry's delivery. She cupped her hands around her eyes to block the glare of the sun and peered out of the glass pane to see who had approached their place.

Her heart pattered, renewing her energy, and chasing away her aches and pains. Luke tied up his steed, an elegant dappled gray quarter horse, the perfect accompaniment to the distinguished gentleman who happened upon their door. She'd seen the tailored cut of a similar suit through the paned glass of a city mercantile before they headed west.

A heavy sigh rumbled from Cora. She looked down, pulling the fullness of her skirt out, hiding the scuffed toes of her worn boots from sight. The threadbare cotton she wore was no match for Luke's custom-fit wool. She considered changing into her best frock, but her waist hadn't shrunk back to its normal twenty-two inches. Dropping her skirt, she patted the loose ringlets too stubborn to be secured in the braid hanging down her back.

Such silliness. She shook her head. The fact she didn't own a black dress didn't mean she wasn't mourning the loss of her husband. "Forgive me, Lord. I meant no dishonor to Hank's memory. I'll get back to my work now. Amen."

Yet, like a disobedient child, she didn't move from the window. She watched Bertha drying her hands on her apron as she walked from the sod house where she washed the railroad men's clothes. By the animation on Luke's chiseled features, she could tell they exchanged pleasantries, even though Bertha's face remained etched with unhappiness.

When Bertha cocked her head toward their home, Luke turned on his heels, striding with confidence toward the house. The beat of Cora's heart turned from a giddy patter to a rapid-fire pace. She placed a hand on her chest. The action didn't steady the beat, or her breathing. She moved from the window to open the door.

She passed by the rectangular table. Her freshly laundered one-piece apron was draped over a chair. Quickly, she tied it around her waist. The blue calico did more than protect her clothing; it added color to her outfit and covered her worn dress.

Hand trembling, she opened the door.

The frosty March morning had turned into a glorious afternoon. The breeze danced with the scent of sun-warmed ground and the promise of spring. Patchy mounds of crusted snow, the only remains of winter's thumbprint, dotted the farmyard. Closing the door to keep the still chilly air from hitting Henry and giving him colic, Cora hugged her body with one arm while lifting the other to shield her eyes from the glare of the sun.

"Afternoon, ma'am." Luke strode toward the door, tipping his bowler.

"Good day, Mr. Dow. Please call me Cora." She lowered her hand when he grabbed a column and swung up onto the porch.

Taking the hand he offered, surprise hiccupped from her when he covered their clasped hands with his free hand.

Luke knitted his brows for a second then broke into a smile. "Only if you will call me Luke."

Sincerity filled his dark brown eyes. The warmth bursting onto her cheeks had nothing to do with the midafternoon sun. She looked down, nodding her head in small jerks.

"It's settled then." Luke released her hand. "Bertha says you have my washing and ironing ready."

"Yes." Cora looked up. She'd completely forgotten this wasn't a social visit. "Please come inside." She reached for the doorknob. Luke beat her to it. She smiled and acknowledged the gesture before stepping into the warmth of the house.

Luke stopped in front of the door. His eyes roved the area by the cookstove where Henry had slept the night of his birth. "Where is that fine boy of yours?"

Cora waved her hand toward the bureau. "I'll get your things."

"No hurry." Luke strode over to where the baby slept, the thud of his boots no match for her thundering heart.

"This is quite the cradle." His laugh filled the house, making the room brighter than it had been in months.

"Many babies' first beds are bureau drawers." Truth be told Hank didn't get the cradle made before his death, but Cora didn't want to talk about that. The happiness Luke brought with him made the air inside fresher than the spring breeze outside.

Luke stroked Henry's cheek with his knuckle then turned shining eyes to Cora. "I hoped he'd be awake to see if he had his ma's pretty green eyes."

Again, Cora's cheeks flamed, this time she turned from Luke's gaze. "It's too soon to tell, I think. They start out blue." She stuffed her hands in her apron pockets, worrying the fringed inner seam.

Heavy footfalls sounded behind her, and she turned to find Luke moving toward her. "Let me check the wood box for you. I can fill it while I'm here. We wouldn't want Henry catching a chill."

"That isn't necessary, Luke. Besides you're in your fancy suit."

"My work clothes are here." Luke looked around their cozy home. "Somewhere."

*This is no way to run a business.* Cora chided herself. She'd have given any other customer his clean laundry by now.

"Let me get them." She squeezed past Luke to the curtained-off pantry. Lifting his pillowcase stuffed with two pairs each of work shirts and trousers from one of the shelves, Cora turned to brush past the burlap curtain. A loaf of bread caught her eye. Without thinking, she grabbed it. She'd offer him an afternoon snack to get him to stay longer.

*Cora! What are you thinking?*

She hesitated, placing the bread back on the shelf. She glanced toward the curtained doorway leading to the room Luke's presence lit up. It would only be hospitable to offer him sustenance. She grabbed the loaf, striding from the pantry before her conscience could stop her.

Luke hovered over the open drawer, staring down at her sleeping son.

Cora set the bread on the warming shelf of the cookstove. "Here you are." She held the pillowcase horizontally at arm's length.

"Still not awake." Disappointment etched Luke's features. With light steps he walked to Cora, slipping his hand under the center of the laundry package, lifting it from her palms. "How much do I owe you?"

"No charge." Cora's hands remained midair, holding nothing. Not knowing what to do with them, she ran them down her apron before locking them together behind her back. "It's my way of saying thank you for your kindness in my time of distress."

The toe of Luke's boot began to bounce. His eyes, which moments before had stared into hers, now roved the wall behind her.

"It was truly a blessing sent by God." Nervous, her words hurried off her tongue.

In a flash, Luke's stare bore down on her, distress veiled the sparkle of his irises. "It was the decent thing to do. God had no part in it."

The disgust in his voice startled her. She caught the gasp of surprise in her throat and swallowed it down. Luke was such a fine man, surely he was a believer. She dropped her gaze to his wiggling boot toe, scrunching the cotton of her apron and full skirt with her hands. "Well, please accept this gift. It's the only way I can say thank you."

"Cora." Luke's voice once again, even and gentle. "I don't want to be beholding to anyone."

Slowly, she raised her head. "Neither do I."

A high-pitched groan sounded from the bureau. Luke turned, stretching his neck to see Henry. "He's only dreaming."

When Luke turned back to Cora, a smile lit up his face. "Let's compromise. I will accept your gift." He raised his hand, lifting the laundry to a further height. "And I'll make the first donation to Henry's future, two bits." His two dark brows lifted in question.

"That sounds quite fitting." Cora smiled at Luke.

With two fingers, Luke dug into his vest pocket pulling out a shiny coin. He turned, walked to the bureau and laid it on top. "You can be one of the first customers at the bank."

"Bank?" What on earth was Luke talking about? She hadn't realized she'd spoken out loud until Luke turned around, his face scrunched. After a few seconds, happy laughter danced through the house.

"The railroad announced the location of the terminus." He strode to the table, setting the pillowcase down. Pulling the straight-back chair, with the slats that Cora had loosened, from under the table, he set it at a slant. Standing behind it, he motioned with his hand for her to sit down.

She obliged. Luke repeated the motion with another chair before sitting opposite her. "The railroad is building the terminus a mile south of your homestead. From what I can tell by looking at their plat maps, your land borders the railroad's property. Did you know that?"

Wide-eyed, Cora shook her head, uncertain what that meant. If the look on Luke's face was any indication, it was good news.

"Your land value just increased."

Cora knew what *that* meant. Their homestead sat on a prime piece of property. She wrung her hands and forced a smile to her face. How she wished they'd proven up already! The extra supplies they needed to survive the hard winter had depleted their meager savings.

This news meant she'd have to work harder than ever to prove up this land. Gaining the deed secured her family's future. She sighed. She and Bertha had been working day and night just to scrape by.

"You need to take a ride to the south border of your land. People have flocked to the area, including me. We're living in tents and some of us have dropped shingle bundles on the ground where we hope to build our businesses."

Excitement and fear wrestled inside of Cora. She lifted her palms to her cheeks. This news might mean she and Bertha could easily prove up or it could mean the opposite.

Luke reached out, removing Cora's hands from her cheeks. His tingling warmth burned through her skin, sending joyous shivers up her arms. "I think this is a grand opportunity for your washing business. I urge you to consider going into town to visit with these future business owners. Most are gentlemen who won't have time to tend their washing and ironing."

Cora nodded. She squeezed Luke's hand. "I will." God was certainly answering her prayers. She longed to share this with Luke. However, based on his earlier reaction, she felt the subject might spoil the moment.

The door burst open. Bertha bustled inside, Clement Dykstra close on her heels.

"What's going on in here?" Anger puckered the pleasant expression Bertha had worn when she came through the door. Clement's face mirrored Bertha's, casting a sinister shadow on his already age-weathered features.

Cora pulled her hands from Luke's with such force her chair teetered on the back two legs and threatened to spill her to the floor. Leaning forward and pushing down with her legs, she regained her balance, but not her composure.

"The railroad is building close to our land. Luke was telling me about business opportunities." Her explanation tumbled out like clothespins from an overturned basket.

Clement pushed around Bertha. The large man filled the room. "Nonsense. The railroad will build where towns are established." He wagged a scolding finger at Cora. Anger shadowed his blue eyes, turning his only attractive feature ugly.

"Are you calling me a liar?" Luke stood, his voice held the threat of a fight. His lean body towered a few inches above Clement's husky frame.

Stepping back, Clement narrowed his deep-set eyes. His white, unruly brows almost covered the tapered opening.

"Take a ride to the southern section of Cora's homestead and you'll see. A town is springing up at this moment." Luke stepped forward until the two men were a hand width apart.

Clement took another step back. He rubbed his chin while his eyes scanned the room. He slackened his stance.

"I might do that." Clement held out his hand. "Clement Dykstra. I own the twenty acres east of the Andersons' homestead on the other side of the rock formations." Civility replaced his scolding tone.

Wariness hummed through Cora. She'd never seen Clement back down from a fight. Most of his and her late husband's discussions had turned into arguments. Clement was a man who couldn't be trusted.

Luke's hesitation to shake Clement's hand was evident. Did he sense something about Clement, too?

Finally, Luke grasped Clement's hand. "Luke Dow, soon to be hotel proprietor."

"So you say the railroad's running tracks where?"

The stench of vileness clung to this man and not from lack of bathing or sweat of the brow. Caginess and deceit took many forms. Life had taught Luke how to spot it even in its most disguised state. He'd tread carefully with this one.

"A mile parallel to *Cora's* land." He emphasized her name, a reminder to this snake about who made the decisions regarding the property.

"And the town springing up is where?"

Anger growled in the pit of Luke's stomach. Clement was trying to trip him up. "A mile south of here. Why don't you hop on your horse and go take a look?" Luke jerked his head toward the door.

"Mr. Dow, Clement is a welcomed guest in our home." Bertha's curt tone turned all their heads and started a small ruckus coming from the bureau drawer.

Cora slipped from her chair. Clement's hungry eyes followed her movements while she crossed the room. A blossom of anger pushed through the lonely chambers of Luke's heart.

"So, you've had the babe." Clement's sickening tone roiled Luke's stomach. The old wolf appeared to be licking his chops over the young lamb.

"This is Henry." Cora lifted Henry in the cradle of her arms to show Clement.

Big, bright blue eyes, the color of his grandma's, peeked from the shadows of the quilt. Luke's heart softened. He smiled until he saw Clement's nostril flare from the slight sneer of his lip. Thankfully, both Bertha and Cora's pride-filled eyes were on little Henry.

"Yes, a fine boy."

Clement's unfeeling tone stoked Luke's anger and distrust. The fingers of his right hand curled into a fist.

Bertha's beaming smile stretched from ear to ear. "I knew you'd think so. Before long he'll be helping with the chores." She tickled Henry's cheek with her index finger.

"Yes, he will." Clement drummed his sausage fingers on his leg. Caginess glowed in his beady eyes. He moved closer to the trio, placing a meaty hand on Cora's shoulder. His arm draped across her back. "He needs a daddy to teach him how to live off the land."

The snake! Implying he'd make a good father to Henry, a good husband to Cora. Why, he could be her father. Yet, Luke had seen it. A woman needing protection in the West might marry anyone. Men gained wives, and sometimes land, increasing their wealth.

Realization widened Luke's eyes. Had Clement been playing dumb? Did he know about the railroad's plans? Was he trying to get Cora or her land? An urge stronger than anything Luke had ever felt before encouraged him to knock Clement's hand from Cora's body.

He was ready to lash out when Cora's jaw set. She took a large sidestep. Clement's hand dropped limply through the air, slapping against his thigh.

"Cora, don't be rude." Bertha chided, standing beside Clement. Together, they created a unified front.

"It's not rude. I am in mourning." Cora spoke slowly and loudly. "It's not respectful for a man to make advances on a mourning widow."

Without thinking, Luke moved closer to Cora, letting her know she wasn't in this alone.

"I beg your pardon." Clement's stiff partial bow and smile didn't fool Luke.

Clement wanted Cora or her land or both. The thought turned Luke's stomach. Cora was a lovely woman. A man would be crazy not to want her, but Clement reminded Luke of his father. This wasn't a good thing.

"I'm doing what the Good Book says, taking care of widows. I know how trying it can be for a woman who's given birth, so I will forgive you for this little incident." Clement tipped his head in a mock bow of apology.

Luke inched closer to Cora, almost lifting a protective arm to her shoulder. What was he thinking? None of this was any of his concern. He'd come to this area to start a business, make his fortune and secure his future. The last thing he wanted to do was get involved with this family. Yet, he couldn't leave with Clement in the house.

"Sir." Luke gave his most respectful nod. "Perhaps this is a good time for us to take leave and ride to the site where the town will be built. You can see the progress with your own eyes." Spending time with Clement was the last thing Luke wanted to do, but if it got him out of Cora's house Luke could endure.

"Splendid idea, young man." Clement turned to Bertha. "When do you think my washing will be ready?"

A soft pat on Luke's lower arm drew his attention to Cora. She mouthed the words *thank you* before she gave him a shy smile.

"Day after tomorrow."

"Well, good afternoon, ladies. I'll see you in a couple of days." Clement lumbered across the floor, stopping at the doorway to wait for Luke.

*Guess I'll be stopping by in couple of days.* Luke took a last look at Henry, and as if the baby could read his mind, Henry smiled.

# Chapter 4

In order to be present when Clement stopped to pick up his washing and ironing, Luke arrived at the Anderson homestead in time to watch daybreak unfold. The upper tip of the sun peeked over the horizon, shooting dazzling colors through the darkness, and lighting the sky with the promise of a sunny spring day.

He'd spent the last three days traveling the proximity of Cora's property. As an outsider, he could see why Bertha thought Clement the perfect suitor for her daughter-in-law. Clement's large two-story house, barn and rolling grassland filled with cattle was impressive.

But with its one-room house, shedlike barn, and rock-lined pasture dotted with sheep, Cora's homestead was far more developed than the two bordering Clement's and the railroad's lands. Both of those properties had sod houses, smaller than the one on Cora's property, with tiny lean-tos on the sides of the structures instead of barns. About a half-dozen cows grazed in a tiny fenced-in pasture on one homestead. The extent of the other neighbor's livestock appeared to be a wagon team and a milk cow.

Guiding his horse to the hitching post by Cora's barn, Luke slid out of the saddle. The warm southerly breezes coaxed green shoots from the ground. He surveyed the landscape around the house, soddy and barn. The well, the anchor Hank Anderson had built his farm around, sat in the middle of the yard, almost an equal distance from each the buildings, centralized to make carrying water to each location easier.

The stretch of land between the sod house and the square-framed barn would work well for a garden. In his idle time, Luke formulated a plan. If the ladies of the house agreed, he'd have a good reason to be on the premises from sunup to sundown on the days Clement made his rounds.

He looped the reins around the rough wood of the post and carefully slipped a burlap bag from the saddle horn. He stepped up onto the porch, glad a faint light shone through the window.

Cora's hushed voice tones emanated from the home, her words flowing steadily. He couldn't make out what she was saying, but he guessed she was reading aloud. Relieved the women were up and had started the day, he lifted his hand and softly knocked on the door. He held the burlap bag tight, hoping they hadn't started their breakfast preparations.

The house grew quiet. Soft footfalls passed the door and movement at the window curtain caught his eye. He smiled at Cora's caution at not opening the door in the early-morning hours.

The glass doorknob turned and the door creaked open. Cora peeked around the corner. Her hand tightly clasped a quilt under her chin, covering her from head to toe. Her

eyes, wide with wonder, searched his face. "Luke, is something wrong?"

"No." His voice croaked. He pushed the burlap bag toward her. "I...um..." Luke's heart leapt in his chest. He'd lost
his train of thought. Curls framed Cora's face and sleepi-
ness veiled her lovely green eyes, inviting him to cup her
cheek in his hand.

Luke grimaced at his inappropriate actions this morning.
He hadn't thought about the women being in their intimate
apparel and not ready to receive visitors. His only concern
had been to offer a barrier against Clement's advances.

Cora raised her eyes from the bag he held out and arched
her brows. "Laundry?"

"Oh, no." Luke pushed the bag closer to Cora. "A slab
of bacon and four eggs."

Pleasure squeaked from Cora. "Eggs. We haven't had
any eggs since the start of winter when a coyote got into
the henhouse."

Bertha peeked over Cora's shoulder. "Who is out there?"

"It's Luke Dow, ma'am. I've brought fixings for breakfast."

"Bacon and *eggs*." Cora pushed the door open wider,
but never relieved Luke of his burden.

"Why?" Bertha pushed in front of Cora. She wore a
heavy coat. The faded blue ruffle of her flannel gown
stopped at her ankle. Her scuffed shoes stuck out from
underneath the hem.

Before Luke could answer, Bertha wrapped her hand
around the top of the bag right above Luke's. Her rough
skin chafed his fingers. She pulled the bag inside the door.
"Are you going to answer me?"

"Yes, ma'am. May I come in?" Luke removed his hat.

"No, we aren't decent." Bertha pushed Cora back. "You
can pump and carry water to the soddy. Pour it into the

cast-iron cauldron and start a fire under it. We'll dress for the day and start breakfast."

"Bertha, Luke is our guest, not our servant." Cora stepped forward, the quilt slipping from her head. A mass of glorious curls tumbled over her forehead and framed her face.

"I know." Bertha's terseness drew Luke's eyes from Cora. "I'm giving him something to do while he waits. He can't come in here while we dress."

"No, but you are telling him to do our work when he has brought us breakfast." Cora turned an apologetic look to Luke.

He held up his palms. "No, Bertha is right. I came too early. I'd be happy to carry and heat the water." *And brush your hair.*

Surprise at his thoughts caught in Luke's throat. He gave Cora a tight smile, turned and stepped quickly off the porch. Yesterday, sitting in his tent, this plan had seemed solid. It gave him a good reason to spend more time on the homestead and keep his eye on Clement.

Cora was a pretty girl. He would allow himself to acknowledge the fact, then he must stop his wandering thoughts about the feel of her silky hair and porcelain skin. He remembered her sleepy-eyed look and sighed. It'd be wonderful to gaze into her pretty green eyes over coffee.

*Enough.* He chided himself. Good thing Bertha had assigned him a chore. He needed some physical work to bring his wandering thoughts back to reality. He came to make a proposition, nothing more. His intentions were neighborly, unlike Clement's.

Striding to the well, Luke pumped the iron handle several times before water sloshed out the spigot and into the bucket.

Luke looked over his shoulder at the house. The morning sun reflected off the glass of the windows. Had the women dressed and started breakfast? Perhaps he'd awakened little Henry, who no doubt demanded a dry diaper and his breakfast.

The slosh of water hitting the wood startled Luke. He looked down at the wet boards covering the well opening. He'd let his mind wander.

He shouldn't even care about Clement's actions toward Cora. It was none of his business. Still, there was something about Clement that reminded Luke of his own father, a man with an ill temper. If Clement acted the way his father did, Luke couldn't allow Cora to get involved with him—no matter what Bertha wanted. Cora was a fine woman, and she had a wonderful baby.

The image of Cora holding Henry the night of his birth popped into Luke's mind. Her sweet face beamed with love as she cradled her son. Her green eyes filled with love and pride.

His disgusted grunt echoed around the farmyard. He needed to take his mind off Cora. He knew how to do that: good hard work.

Luke refocused his attention on the brimming bucket.


"Cora, what is taking you so long?" The thud of a chunk of wood dropping into the cookstove punctuated Bertha's impatient voice.

Looking into the mirror on the washstand, Cora considered her hair. She longed for straight hair that would lay smooth from her center part. Instead, short stubborn ringlets coiled around her face like sprung bedsprings.

Sighing, she brushed through her hair one more time, knowing full well she couldn't control her curls. Instead she tried to bring out its natural shine. Cora separated her waist-length hair into three sections and quickly braided them together. She rolled the thick braid to the base of her neck and secured it with her ivory combs, hair accessories far too dressy for a normal workday, but between Luke's presence and bacon and eggs for breakfast, the day felt special.

She leaned close to the washbasin mirror, pinching her cheeks to give them color. Henry's birth had taken a lot out of her. Although her body was returning to normal, her skin remained pale.

Cora grabbed her blue apron from the peg on the pantry wall and carefully slipped it over her head. She pushed her arms through the shoulder straps and stepped through the privacy curtain.

"I'm sorry I'm running behind this morning." Cora gathered a swaddled and screaming Henry from Bertha's shoulder.

"Only one small burp." Bertha sighed and pulled a cast-iron fry pan from the warmer shelf and set it on the flat surface of the stove.

Cora's shoulders and heart drooped. She wanted to talk to Luke, not deal with Henry's colic today. Angling her son in a vertical position with his head resting on her shoulder, Cora paced the floor and patted his back.

She felt his little body clench. Poor little thing.

*Please forgive me, Lord, for putting my pleasure before my son's comfort.*

A whimper cut through the sudden silence of the room.

Bertha cupped Henry's head with her hand when she walked by. "I see so much of your father in you." She leaned in, pecking his chubby cheek before returning to her work. She carried three blue enamel mugs and utensils to the table.

"I can do that." In a week's time, Cora had mastered setting the table while holding Henry, not to mention sweeping and dusting and other chores. She grinned. Dealing with colic was a challenge, but worth every minute because it meant she still had a family. She stopped laying the table-ware, looked down at her son's pixie face, and gave him a tight hug.

His little tummy thumped against her, then he released a loud hiccup of air. His lips pulled into a slight smile.

"Oh you think that's funny, do you?" Cora held Henry at arm's length. She puffed out her cheeks, wrinkled her nose and made a little clicking noise, hoping to incite a real smile rather than a gas-induced grin.

Laughter bounced through the rafters—Luke's laughter, not Henry's. Heat burst onto Cora's cheeks and she stopped making the face. Luke continued laughing as he stepped backward, closing the door with his shoulder.

Cora pulled Henry close, wishing she could hide her face in his blanket. "I didn't hear you at the door."

Looking from her to the baby, joy shined in Luke's eyes. "Good morning."

"Good morning." Cora mumbled her greeting while resuming her one-handed place setting. She lowered her head to hide her embarrassed flush.

"It smells wonderful in here."

Luke's heavy footsteps approached the table.

"Bertha made a batch of biscuits—our contribution to breakfast." Cora stole a quick glance at him then returned to nervously adjusting the tableware.

"This is quite a treat for us," Bertha said as she laid a piece of bacon in the hot pan.

The bacon sputtered and sizzled before releasing a smoky aroma. Cora's mouth watered. She missed pork and beef. Although mutton was delicious, it grew tiresome eating it for every meal. If she started an actual laundry business, the first thing she planned to buy was a few chickens and pigs to expand their larder.

She'd turned Luke's suggestion of starting a laundry

business over and over in her mind. Even though it was a task most women could easily perform, she and Bertha had something the other homesteads didn't: clear water.

Hank had drilled for days, pulling up buckets full of sand before he hit crystal-clear water. He thought the sand must have purified it or he had hit a natural spring. The other landowners around them dug wells and found water all right, but it was rust-red water that stained clothes, especially whites.

She'd been praying to God to help her and Bertha keep their homestead and felt the location of the town and starting a laundry business might be the answer to her prayers.

"How should I cook your eggs, Mr. Dow?"

"Any way but burnt, ma'am. I'm afraid I'm not much of a cook. And please call me Luke."

Cora glanced at Luke. Scrambled eggs would go further; however, it'd been a long time since she'd eaten an over-easy yolk. "Perhaps over easy. Luke could have two, leaving one for each of us?"

A slight grimace drew the corner of Luke's mouth down. "How about over hard for me?"

Bertha gave a nod. "Not a dipper?"

His wrinkled-nose answer was so endearing, Cora's heart fluttered, sending a new flush to her cheeks.

"Please have a seat." Cora adjusted Henry on her hip.

"I need to wash up first." Luke stepped toward the pantry. "May I?"

"Of course." Cora followed him, placing Henry in the basket beside the warm cookstove. She wanted to seek Luke's counsel on the washing business. She'd considered the advantages and disadvantages. She knew she'd need Bertha's help to make it a success. Yet, Cora hadn't spoken to Bertha about it for fear she'd nix the idea.

"The biscuits should be ready." Bertha moved to the

side of the oven door while Cora grabbed a heavy towel to slip a small cast-iron pan from the hot oven. The golden-crusted treat rose high in the pan.

She inhaled their buttery scent and carried them over to the table. Moving the family Bible to the side, she placed the biscuits in the center of the table.

The swish of burlap and the scuff of boot heels sent her heart reeling. Luke's presence today had a strong effect on her. She needed to muster her courage to consult with him about starting a business and steel her resolve for Bertha's arguments against the idea. She must conquer her silly emotions. It wasn't proper mourning behavior and her emotions might get in the way of her concerted effort to establish a permanent home for their family.

She turned. Luke scooped Henry's basket from the floor.

"You, little man, need to join us at the table." He gently swung the basket back and forth, taking careful steps across the floor.

His awkward movements were comical, but his sincere wish to include Henry in their meal curved her lips into a wide smile and sent her heart into a jig-time dance.

"Haven't you ever seen a baby before?" Bertha gave her head a shake and held out two filled plates.

Cora stepped around Luke, taking the plates from Bertha.

"I haven't. Well, I have seen babies before, just not this close." Luke made faces at Henry.

Cora bit the corner of her lip to keep from laughing. She made a wide berth around Luke and the swaying basket to set the plates on the table.

Luke followed her to the table and sat down on the same chair he'd used when he shared supper with them the night Henry was born. He placed the basket beside his chair.

Cora set the plate with two eggs in front of Luke. She

stepped around the basket and placed the other plate on the table. She intended to sit beside Luke. She pulled her hand across the chair slats to pull it out.

Bertha swatted it away and pushed the plate she held at Cora. "You're not sitting in my chair." She slid onto the seat.

Drawing a deep breath, Cora pursed her lips and carried her breakfast to the seat across the table from Luke.

He turned his attention from Henry and looked directly into Cora's eyes. Mirth glimmered in his brown irises.

Bertha cleared her throat. Hating to break their connection, Cora dropped her eyes, clasped her hands and bowed her head as Bertha prayed.

"Heavenly Father, thank You for this fine food we are about to receive. Bless us this day. Let our hands and hearts serve You. Amen."

"Amen." Cora's murmur echoed Bertha. She knitted her brows. Perhaps Luke said a silent amen. When she opened her eyes, though, Luke's attention was back on Henry.

"Help yourself to a biscuit." Cora nodded to the pan. "You are out early this morning."

"I'll say. You interrupted our Bible reading." Bertha handed Luke the crock of butter.

"Begging your pardon, ma'am." Luke tipped his head while slathering his biscuit with butter. "With so much time on my hands waiting around in town, I came up with an idea that could benefit all of us and I was anxious to talk to you about it."

"Is it about a laundry?" Cora blurted out.

Bertha scowled at her. "What?"

"Well, no." Luke's brows pulled together, wrinkling his forehead. "It's about a garden and chickens. There are some folks in town planning to open a general store. They have seeds and chickens for sale. I want to buy some, but until they announce the town site and plot it out, I have no place for either and I'll need both for my hotel." Luke stopped and devoured half his biscuit in one bite.

"You plan to serve food at your hotel?" Cora interlocked her fingers and rested her chin in them.

"We had chickens. Coyotes or raccoons got them this winter," Bertha said, setting the butter crock down with a thump.

"I think I can build a sturdy coop for them. You have a perfect spot for a garden between the barn and the sod house." Luke scooped some of his eggs from his plate. He looked at Cora. "Aren't you going to eat?"

Cora looked down at her untouched breakfast. She'd been mesmerized by Luke's ambition. "Yes, I am." She poked her yolk with her fork, thick golden goodness oozed down the browned egg white. If they had a henhouse again, this meal would be a staple rather than a treat.

"Do you have a plow? Most of the frost should be out of the ground. I could get started breaking the soil today." Luke's bacon snapped when he took a bite.

"Why would we move our garden plot?" Bertha smacked her lips, cutting another bite of her egg.

"I didn't know you had a garden plot." Luke lifted his mug.

"We forgot to pour the coffee." Cora stood and hurried to the stove.

"It's out behind the priv..."

"Bertha," Cora scolded. "We are in mixed company." She walked carefully across the floor with the hot coffee-pot, avoiding Henry's basket. "Our small garden is behind the house."

Luke's lip curled into a smile. "I was thinking of raising a large garden, enough to fill two pantries—yours and my hotel's."

"I don't think the spot is big enough." Cora reached

across the table and poured coffee into Luke's mug. She filled Bertha's, then hers before setting the pot on the table.

"Well, it would be easier to plow since the ground's been broken. If you're agreeable to the notion, I'll take a look after breakfast."

Cora looked to Bertha. She frowned and gave her head a small shake.

"We have to plant a garden anyway. It would be nice to have help weeding and harvesting." Cora laid a hand on her mother-in-law's arm. "I intend to prove up this homestead, not return to the East."

"I know." Bertha narrowed her eyes at Cora. "You have someone else to consider and he wouldn't think too highly of letting another man tend your garden."

Cora's stomach flip-flopped at Bertha's double meaning. She drew her hand back. How could she make her mother-in-law see she had no intention of marrying Clement? Ever. Her disdain for him bubbled in her throat. She swallowed hard before continuing.

"As a matter of fact..." Cora cleared her throat and looked at Luke. "I want to talk to you about starting a laundry business in that new town you're so excited about."

Bertha gasped and brought a hand to her chest. "Running a business is a man's job."

"We already take in washing and ironing." Cora stole a glance at Luke. His affirmative nod fortified her resolve.

"We were temporarily washing the railroad men's clothes to give us enough money to make it through the winter. Otherwise, we only do our own and Clement's." Bertha scooted her chair back. The hard scrape prompted a startled cry from Henry.

Cora pursed her lips and started to rise. Luke leaned down and scooped Henry out of the basket. He rested her son's head in the crook of his arm then sat in a precariously tense position.

"You shouldn't wait until the exact location is announced. You should make a trip into town now. There is a need for a laundry service. The gentleman who hopes to get the property beside me is a barber. He is interested in bringing his laundry out to you, and he is not the only one. Between me and the railroad men, we've stirred quite a bit of interest in your fine work."

Bertha stood by the cookstove, her back to the table, and grunted before she turned. "This is not a good idea. You need to discuss it with Clement."

A flicker of anger ran through Luke's eyes. He set his jaw and gave his head a slight shake.

Although Cora didn't know Luke well, she valued his opinion. His clothes and actions reflected his head for business. She squared her shoulders and stood.

"I plan to prove up this claim and make our farm a success. In order to do that, we need food and money. Luke, plow up whatever land you think is best for a garden. Tomorrow I'll take the wagon to the proposed town site and offer our services for washing and ironing."

Bertha's pinched face showed her disdain for Cora's opinion, while Luke's wide smile and nod supported her decision. Cora's stomach flip-flopped.

In a good way.

## Chapter 5

Cora held her arms out straight from her sides for balance while she placed one foot in front of the other and walked on the two-foot-high rock foundation in the far pasture. Last spring, Hank had set the stone base for a twenty-by-thirty building, using loose stones found around the rocky crags that jutted through this area of their property as well as rocks the plow turned up when preparing the soil for their garden.

The walls and roof were to have been their summer work. Hank had wanted this barn finished by the time they proved up. He'd had big plans for their spread and Cora was determined to see them through, although she scrapped the idea of raising this barn.

Jumping down from the rock foundation, Cora rubbed the chill from her nose with the back of her rough work glove. She inhaled the warm spring air. Holding its freshness in her lungs, she bent down and scooped more sheep droppings into a bucket.

As she straightened, she exhaled. When she'd agreed to a larger, shared garden she didn't realize it would include such a horrible task. But Luke insisted working the waste into the soil would help their plants grow. He'd plowed their old garden spot and was halfway done breaking the ground between the barn and the sod house. He wanted to work the sheep droppings into the soil on the second tilling.

Luke planned to plant potatoes in the spot behind the house, insisting the ground had to be ready to plant by Good Friday. To Cora's surprise, Bertha agreed with him. With the date fast approaching, Cora spent a good share of each morning following behind and picking up after her flock.

Spring brought several new additions to her herd of sheep, but winter's fierceness and nature's predators had thinned their flock considerably. Hank had butchered a few of their livestock before he took ill, and moved the rest of them to what he felt was a more protected area close to the barn.

Unfortunately, through their mourning and her pregnancy, she and Bertha could barely manage to water and feed the flock. The sheep broke through the fenced area and wandered around their property. What Hank planned as their livelihood was now a meager number, twenty-five head.

That's why establishing the washing and ironing business was so important. Luke was correct about a need for washing and ironing. The day she went to the site where many hoped the town would be built, she came back with three bags of wash. In two weeks, the number of their customers doubled.

Cora bent down with the scoop. The sheep started to bleat and move around. Slowly straightening, she locked her gaze on the rock formations that surrounded them on three sides. Was a mountain lion nearby? She breathed deeply. The only scent she detected was her flock.

Warily, she carried the bucket to the wagon. Her horse seemed unfazed, yet the sheep continued their nervous stirring. Then she saw the cause, a lone rider easing his horse down a rocky slope. Had she been gone so long Luke looped around her land looking for her?

She squinted, trying to make out the rider. The hair on the back of her neck stood. Cora lifted her skirts and climbed into the buckboard. She needed to get her horse pointed for home. Although she was only a quarter of a mile from the house, the area was isolated by the rock formations. There was no mistaking the portly stature of the man in the saddle. Clement.

"Giddyup." She held the reins and released the brake on the wagon. Slowly, the black draft horse began to walk. She needed to get through the opening and around the bend of the rocks.

"Cora."

Clement's shout bounced off the rock formation, and the repeating echo of his voice calling her name chilled her blood. Fear shot through her. The way he looked at her made her skin crawl. She didn't trust him. The last thing she wanted was to be alone with Clement. Teeth clenched, she snapped the leather against the horse's hind quarters. "Giddyup, Dutch."

Dutch shook his head, making the reins vibrate in her hands as he picked up his pace. Cora laced the leather straps through her fingers so she wouldn't lose her grip and guided Dutch in a wide turn. They started on the path toward home. The rocky trail made it hard to drive the wagon very fast and she couldn't afford to break a wagon wheel.

"Whoa. Whoa up there, pony." Clement rode up beside her.

She clicked her tongue and snapped the reins. She stole a side glance at Clement. He was inspecting the load in the box of her wagon.

"What are you up to out here all alone?"

His tone magnified her fear. He rode closer to the wagon, reaching for the lead line to pull Dutch to a stop.

"I've got to get home. It's time to feed Henry." Cora wiggled her reins, making them difficult for Clement to grab.

"You're not being very neighborly." Clement snapped. The hand he'd reached out came back with a palm full of air.

Cora tugged the reins. Dutch veered slightly to the right, putting some distance between the wagon and Clement. They were close to rounding the crag. The homestead would shortly be in sight.

Narrowing her eyes, Cora looked at Clement. "I told you it's time to feed Henry."

"The babe can wait." The gleam in Clement's eyes roiled her stomach. He guided his horse next to the wagon, reaching for her arm.

*Dear God, I am afraid. Please comfort me, steady me and help me get home safely. Amen.* Although Cora mouthed the words, her petition remained between her and God.

She moved her feet, braced them hard to hold her balance and scooted to the opposite edge of the wagon seat.

"Playing hard to get are you?" Clement snarled and turned his horse to loop behind the wagon. "I'll take that out of you. I want an obedient woman."

Every muscle in Cora's body tensed. A few more feet and she'd be around the bend, yet if she didn't make it... Cora shivered at the thought as she slid to the opposite side of the wagon seat, snapping the reins with such force that Dutch's whinny sounded like a roar.

"I've had enough of this." Clement spurred his steed, passing the wagon.

He was going to try to block her path, stop Dutch in his tracks. She grimaced. "Sorry, Dutch." She snapped the reins. Her startled horse took off at a run. The wagon wheels found every rock, jarring her body with each bounce. She fought to hold the reins tight.

Clement rode faster, turning his horse right before the bend in the path then rode straight toward the wagon.

Her breath came hard. Dutch's pace slowed. Cora surveyed her options, she could jump off the wagon and run, but she'd never outrun or outclimb Clement's horse. It'd do her no good to holler for help, the rocky crags would block her shouts. She had to get around the formations, out into the open prairie.

The closer he rode, the wider Clement's evil smile became. Her heart hammered in her chest. She glanced around the wagon for anything to help her get away. All she had was buckets full of her hard work this morning.

Swinging a full bucket and knocking Clement from his horse might buy her some time, allow her to get closer to home. Holding the reins with one hand, she reached over the buckboard seat, trying to catch the rope handle of a bucket. Her fingertips brushed the scratchy hemp. She couldn't quite grasp it.

"You're mine now." Clement's high-pitched laugh echoed through the rocks, the stench of his intentions stronger than the load of manure in her wagon.

Her heart threatened to leap from her chest, it pounded so hard. Cora stretched her arm to no avail. She couldn't reach the rope handle of the bucket. Her best chance was staying with the wagon. She couldn't let Clement get close enough to get the reins to grab them. She'd have to circle Dutch around and attempt another escape. She braced her feet against the wood. It was risky. The buckboard might tip over, but it was the only thing she could do. She started to pull the reins to guide Dutch into a tight left when she saw him.

Luke's horse loped around the rocky crag, and before she could call for help, Luke's heels touched his horse's sides, sending it into a full gallop.

"What's going on here?" Luke abruptly stopped his horse beside the wagon. The gray stallion snorted and danced on its back legs until it stood flush with the buckboard.

Terror etched every pretty feature of Cora's face. Her breath heaved from her. Loose, wild curls framed her face.

Clement stopped his horse on the opposite side of the wagon, jutted out his chin, and quirked an eyebrow. "I don't believe I care for your tone or the insinuation in your question."

Cora slid away from Clement with wide-eyed fear.

Anger slithered through Luke. He had a good idea what the weasel was up to. "I'd appreciate an answer all the same."

The flush of fear faded from Cora's skin. Replaced by the same bleached-sheet pallor as the day she gave birth to Henry.

Leaning over his saddle horn, Clement gave Cora a sly smile. "Why, I was trying to save myself some miles and give *Mrs. Anderson* my weekly laundry."

Cora jerked her head toward Luke. The panic in her eyes and the quiver of her lips conveyed the truth.

"That's not how it looked to me." Luke guided his horse around the back of the wagon, stopping beside Clement.

Unless his laundry was invisible, which wasn't probable, Clement was lying. If he wasn't dropping off his wash, what was he doing out here on Cora's land?

Luke met Clement's angry glower. He intended to get Clement to stop bothering Cora once and for all. "Cora, you head on home now."

He waited for the rattle of the wagon setting into motion. When it didn't come, he turned in his saddle. Cora's body slumped in the seat. Had she fainted? "Cora?"

She lifted her head. Heavy lids covered her pretty green eyes. Then he saw that her hands were shaking. He knew the feeling well, terror's shock waves. He'd crumpled under its force many times. Overwhelming concern for Cora's well-being surged through him. He had to get her home before Clement saw her fall apart.

Keeping his eye on Clement, he dismounted his horse and climbed aboard the wagon. He tied his reins around the brake lever. It'd be slow going leading his horse this way, but it'd give Cora a chance to recover.

Luke unlaced the reins from Cora's fingers, clicked his tongue, and the wagon jerked to life.

"You're going to pay for this." Clement raised his fist into the air. "Both of you."

Cora gasped. Luke hoped Clement didn't hear it. Luke knew too well that men with Clement's temperament used fear to their advantage. He sat straighter, knowing his stance showed Clement his threats held no power over Luke. If only Cora would follow suit.

"Please sit up straight."

Silent tears trickled down Cora's cheeks when she lifted her head. Her brows furrowed.

"Trust me, sit up straight."

She seemed to understand, giving him a small nod. She drew a ragged breath, and squared her shoulders.

It was all Luke could do to drive the wagon out of the

rocky bluffs. Cora sat erect, but still quaked with fear. Somehow he had to check to see if Clement followed them. When they came to the bend in the rutty path, Luke craned his neck. The swish of a horse's tail was all he could see in the distance. Relieved, he allowed his erect shoulders to sag. With the enemy in retreat and the homestead in sight, Luke let Dutch pull the wagon a few more feet.

"It's safe now."

Cora's ramrod back collapsed. She doubled over, head to her knees. Though she made no sound, her body quivered so hard the wagon seat vibrated.

With each beat of his heart, fright rippled through him. Not the same type of terror Cora had experienced a few minutes ago. No, this fear came from the ineptness of knowing how to comfort a woman. He reached out a hand and patted her shoulder before giving it a small squeeze. "You're okay, it's over."

A small squeak answered him when Cora sucked in a breath and leaned toward him.

Luke gave the guide reins a loose loop around the brake handle, certain Dutch knew the way home. "I think you'll feel better if you sit up." He placed his hands on her shoulders and helped her sit up straight.

She moved with his guidance. When she was almost upright she turned her face to his.

"Thank you. What made you come to find me?"

The tears brimming in her eyes and streaking down her face were more than Luke could bear. He looked out to the horizon and wrapped his arm around her shoulders.

"I don't know." Luke didn't want to tell Cora he'd been looking for someone else. He'd been guiding his horse and the plow through the defrosting ground between the sod house and the barn when he got a strong feeling that someone needed help, so he removed the yoke, saddled his horse and rode off to see who needed a helping hand. Seeing no one on the horizon, he'd headed to the bluffs, and arrived just in the nick of time.

"Did you holler for help? Or ask Clement to go?" That must be it. It was the only thing that made any sense.

Her head moved against his shoulder. "No, I just prayed."

Luke tensed at Cora's words. How on earth did she think praying would help her escape? Why Cora believed in such foolishness, he'd never know.

Cora tipped her head back. A peaceful expression settled on her face, yet a strange smile curved her lips. "Thank you."

Her body stopped shaking and melded warm and soft against his side, the bright sunlight no match for the twinkling happiness that danced in her emerald eyes.

He reached out and ran his finger through a wayward curl. Nearing the end of the feathery spiral, he twirled it around his finger. "You're welcome." His response a breathy whisper, he pulled her closer, brushing his lips against her temple.

The coolness of her skin a contrast to the heat on his lips, he trailed light kisses down the side of her cheek, letting go of the curl and running his fingers through her hair. Her soft skin and hair captivated him, urged him to feel the exquisiteness of her lips. He pulled away for a second, wanting to see the warmth of her beautiful eyes before they fluttered closed at the meeting of their lips.

Sadness replaced the happy light Luke expected to see reflected in her eyes. Cora placed her hand on his cheek. "Luke, I'm in mourning. This isn't proper."

## Chapter 6

It'd been a week and Luke hadn't said more than three words to her since he'd interrupted Clement's evil plans. Cora didn't think she'd angered him because he showed up each day and worked to ready their garden spots.

Maybe she'd hurt his pride by not allowing his kiss. If she had, it wasn't her intention. She longed for his kiss. She wanted to kiss him, more than anything at that moment, but it wasn't right—she was still a recent widow. She placed a palm to her cheek. Although the spring morning air was chilly, her skin burned at her improper thoughts.

Cora gave her apron strings a hard tug before looping them into a bow behind her back. Today was her turn to tend to the washing while Bertha ironed and watched Henry. She lifted a wet shirt from the basket and flipped it over the clothesline. She fished a clothespin from her apron pocket and brought it down with more force than necessary to secure the cloth to the taut rope line.

She'd felt so warm and safe in the crook of Luke's arm. Cora sighed. Feeling secure wasn't a good reason to give in to fleeting emotions. After all, she may be partial to Luke, but she didn't really know him well. He never spoke of his family or the home he left behind, only his business and future plans. Besides she could tell they didn't share the same view of God.

Bending, she absentmindedly picked up another wet item and pinned it to the line. He did know about business, though. With Luke's help, they'd strung two more clotheslines. She'd hoped all the lines would be filled on their designated laundry day. So far, that hadn't happened. Most of their clients were railroad men, which made sense because they were being paid—unlike the men who camped out at the proposed town site and shared Luke's dream of building profitable businesses.

Luke believed when the town was built she'd have more customers. She believed God heard her prayers to keep her home and family together and would provide a way to do that in His time and according to His plan.

Cora finished pinning the clothes on the line then lifted the empty basket and walked toward the house. In the distance two riders approached. Panic wrung the moisture from her mouth and squeezed her insides into a tight knot. She took quick steps to the house.

Shielding her eyes from the sun's glare, she saw it wasn't Clement. She recognized Luke's mount and his hat. Relief rinsed away her fear. She stepped up onto the porch and waited for their visitors. Her curiosity was piqued by the stranger riding beside Luke.

"Good morning." She called her cheerful greeting before the men reached the house.

"Hello." Luke's smile seemed warmer and brighter than

the spring sun. He dismounted and walked his horse to the barn. He tied him off and removed his saddle.

The other rider tipped his head when he rode past Cora, following Luke's lead. Brown hair flecked with gray stuck out from under the same type of citified hat Luke wore, but his clothes were more commonplace—trousers and a wool coat.

The men walked toward the house. "Cora Anderson, this is Alford Vernon. He's my campmate."

"Nice to meet you, ma'am." Mr. Vernon, stocky and slightly shorter than Luke, removed his hat and tipped his head, revealing a shiny bald spot ringed by short two-toned hair.

"My pleasure. Will you come in for some coffee?"

"I'm really here on business." Alford worried his hat in his hands. "I came to ask about your laundry services, but..."

"Let's go inside." Cora knew what Mr. Vernon planned to say. She'd heard it before when she'd been to the proposed town site. He had no money. Many of the people asked for credit until the town was built. Cora and Bertha agreed they weren't going to work without payment. They did believe in Christian charity; however, they'd started their venture to help ease the burden of proving up the homestead and they needed to take paying customers.

"I see your skepticism, ma'am." Alford allowed Cora to pass first through the door. Luke followed behind.

Bertha stopped rocking Henry and stood when she saw the visitors trailing behind Cora.

"Bertha, this is Alford Vernon. Mr. Vernon, my mother-in-law, Bertha Anderson."

"It's a pleasure to make your acquaintance, ma'am." Alford gave a slight bow in Bertha's direction.

Luke made a sound that sounded suspiciously like a "Harrumph."

Cora's eyes widened and she stifled a giggle. Bertha's face had changed. A rosy glow touched her cheeks and a mirth-filled smile replaced her tight lips. Cora hadn't seen Bertha's genuine smile since they decided to head west, yet she braced for Bertha's negative reaction to Luke's disbelief.

It never came. She wasn't even sure if Bertha heard it because Bertha hadn't taken her eyes off Alford. She walked up to him and offered her hand. "Thank you. It's nice to meet you, too."

Not knowing what to do, Cora looked to Luke. Merriment filled his eyes. He gave a conspiratorial wink, crossed the room and lifted a wide-awake Henry from Bertha's arms.

"I believe you have some business to discuss." He turned on his heel, walked across the room and folded his lanky frame into the rocking chair.

"What is it we can do for you, Mr. Vernon?" Bertha motioned for him to sit on the nearest chair with one hand and fidgeted with her apron strings with the other. Finally, the bow released and she pulled the apron from her yellow print dress. She smoothed her skirt before sitting down in the chair next to Mr. Vernon.

Stifling a giggle, Cora sat down. "I believe Mr. Vernon..."

"Please call me Al." Alford managed to look away from Bertha and acknowledge Cora.

"I believe Al wants us to do his washing and ironing, but he doesn't have money to pay." Cora raised her eyebrows at Bertha.

"I see." Bertha answered and kept her eyes focused on Al. A touch of sourness crept back into Bertha's expression.

Al looked from Cora to Bertha. "It is a true fact. I don't

have money to spare right now. I need my cash to build a barbershop when they announce the location of the town."

"We don't work on credit." Bertha crossed her arms over her chest.

Cora's deep exhale relaxed her shoulders. For a moment she'd thought Bertha might be taken in by Al's charms.

"Understandably so." Al nodded his head. "I certainly wouldn't cut someone's hair for nothing. I'm quite a good shot and I thought if you'd allow it, I could pay you with pheasants, jackrabbits and quail. They are quite plentiful in these parts."

Cora drew back in her chair. This was new—someone willing to barter for their services. They could use a variety of meats. Since Hank passed, they'd eaten mutton for most their meals. She wished she could catch Luke's eye, read his expression, see if he approved of bartering. "I don't know. We don't want to be picking buckshot out of our meat." Bertha puckered her lips.

"I'm a better shot than that, plus I'll dress the meat for you, too."

Bertha's eyes met Cora's. She lifted her brows and shrugged. Cora knew Bertha approved and was leaving the decision to her. If they started doing this for Al, would they have to barter with other customers?

"Ladies, before you decide." Al held up his hands, palms out. "Let me do a little hunting. Provide the meat for your Sunday dinner. If you are happy with its condition, then perhaps we can make a deal."

"Sunday dinner." Cora closed her eyes and remembered the bustle on Saturday to get all of their work finished so they could observe the Sabbath. Rising early on Sunday, dressing in their finest, and heading out to worship with their neighbors. Then they had headed west and all of that

was in the past. Sometimes she understood Bertha's un-
pleasantness. She missed having a town nearby, too.

Cora cleared her throat. She didn't need Luke's approval.
"What a fine idea, Mr.—" Al interrupted her with a stern
look. "Al." His merry smile rewarded her for agreeing with
his suggestion and using his given name.

"We have a young preacher at the camp. He's starting Sunday services. Would you ladies care to join us for
the church service? I'm afraid it's rustic—blankets on the
ground will be our pews."

A real church service. Cora hesitated to answer. She
wanted to say yes, but after the episode with Clement in
the rocks, she wasn't certain they'd be safe making the
one-mile journey to the site, and this time she'd have little
Henry with her.

She sighed and looked at Bertha. The soft lines of her
face drew a portrait of the same homesickness Cora felt.
They'd both been cooped up too long in the house, working hard to survive. Besides, it'd be nice to hear a sermon.
She and Bertha took turns reading the Bible daily, but a
preacher applied the word to life and gave you something
to ponder all week.

"What a splendid idea. Don't you think so, Bertha?"

"I do. After church, we can all come back to the homestead for Sunday dinner." Bertha grinned from ear to ear.

Cora chuckled at her mother-in-law's excitement. She
turned her gaze to Luke. "A church service with Sunday
dinner afterward will be grand, don't you think?"

Luke answered her question with a dark scowl. Her smile
faded. Luke was a fine man. Surely, he attended worship
services?

A knock sounded at the door. Cora hopped from her
chair and almost skipped across the floor. Even Luke's dark

mood couldn't dampen her excitement. She hadn't realized how much she missed having a town close by.

Distracted by her thoughts, she threw open the door and stood face-to-face with Clement.

"Good morning, Cora." His hunger-filled eyes and smug smile deflated Cora's jubilation.

"Clement." She growled out his name through tightly clenched teeth.

The rocker creaked and heavy footfalls sounded on the floor.

"Well, ask him in." Bertha bustled by her. "I'll put on some coffee."

"That's right neighborly of you," Clement answered Bertha and gave Cora a pointed look.

She stepped away from the door, allowing Clement to enter. She had not told Bertha about the week-old incident by the crags.

"My, what do we have here? A meetinghouse?" Clement chuckled until he noticed Luke's icy stare.

Luke held a sleeping Henry in arms. He motioned for Cora to take her child.

"Do you have washing to pick up?" Anger underlay Luke's even tone, but he gently released Henry into Cora's arms.

"Why I don't think it's any of your business, Mr. Dow."

Bertha turned from the cookstove. "We are making plans for Sunday dinner after church."

*No!* Cora's insides screamed. Hadn't Bertha detected the friction in the house upon Clement's entry?

A low growl sounded in Luke's throat, his tight jaw twitched. "I'm sure Mr. Dykstra has other plans."

"Well, I will be attending church so it's a possibility." Clement raised his eyebrows at Cora.

She took a step back as Luke stepped forward, fists clenched at his sides.

Haughtiness covered Clement's features. He turned and addressed Bertha. "Shall I stop by and give you ladies a ride to church?"

Bertha turned, wiping her palms down her skirt, a wide smile lit up her face. "Why certain..."

"I'm sorry to disappoint you, Clement," Luke interrupted. "They've already agreed to accompany me."

Luke rubbed his eyes with his thumb and forefinger. He should still be fast asleep in his tent, not loping along the path to Cora's homestead.

What was it about her that stirred him? Made him jump to her defense? Made him want to wrap her and Henry in his arms? Protect them from all the badness in the world? She was so determined to keep her homestead. The odds favored failure, even with the short time left on the agreement.

He'd tried to help by urging her to take in laundry. Got her excited about the idea before he realized most of the folks waiting for the railroad's announcement were cash-strapped.

The rising sun shot tinges of pink through the eastern sky. Why on earth did the preacher set the church service at eight o'clock in the morning? Weren't folks supposed to rest on the Sabbath?

Luke blinked his eyes hard in an effort to wake up. When that didn't help, he gave his head a hard shake. His side vision caught a flicker of light by the rocky ledge outlining Cora's homestead.

"Whoa." Luke stretched his body until he stood in the stirrups. The light wasn't low enough for a campfire. It seemed to bob about seven hands high from the ground.

He leaned forward, trying to get a better look. The light seemed to disappear then show up again a few feet away, like a firefly's dance through evening's twilight.

Golden beams brightened the darkness, casting a fiery glow on the jagged crags. The rocks glistened in the sunshine.

Pulling his brows together, Luke sat back in the saddle. He strained his tired eyes. He saw only the splendor of nature, dotted with sheep. He sighed. The sun's reflection had tricked him into thinking he saw a floating flame.

It was nothing. He tapped his heels into his horse and swayed with its gentle movement. He'd gotten too involved with this family, worrying about their well-being when he should be worried about his own. Everyone knew how the world worked—you took care of yourself. You didn't rely on anyone. It was a life lesson he knew well.

Once the railroad announced the location of the town and the construction of his hotel got underway, it'd get his mind off the pretty widow.

Luke's sigh echoed through the silent dawn. He shouldn't have initiated a kiss. He knew she was in mourning. His fear for her safety the day Clement had caught her in the rocky crags overwhelmed him. Holding Cora secure in his arms and sharing a kiss seemed like the natural thing to do.

A soft glow flickered in the homestead window. He rode to the barn, slipped from his horse and began to ready the wagon for the journey back to town. He'd fight his attraction to Cora. Stay focused on his business.

The click of the door and light footfalls broke the quiet of the morning. Luke figured one of the women was making her morning visit to the outhouse. Concern niggled his thoughts. Had someone been out in the rocky terrain? He stopped harnessing Dutch and stepped to the barn door, intending to make sure either Cora or Bertha returned to the house.

Standing in the shadows of the barn, he peered around the door. The image he saw moving across the farmyard made his heart race and took his breath away.

Cora, with the ivory crocheted shawl around her shoulders, crossed the yard carrying a steaming cup of coffee. Her peach dress, though outdated in style, showed off her slender form. No one would believe she'd delivered a baby just six weeks ago. Her hair had been swept up to a coil on top of her head.

His heart pattered with happiness, instantly stretching his mouth into a wide smile. She was a vision of loveliness.

"Good morning." He cleared his throat to remove sleep's rasp from his voice. Who was he kidding? His emotions put the edge in his voice.

"'Morning. I thought you'd enjoy a cup of coffee before heading back into town. I'd ask you in except Bertha's dressing." Cora held the cup out by its handle.

Clasping the lip of the mug, Luke removed it from her hand, never breaking eye contact.

"Much obliged."

He expected Cora to return to the house. She stood firm in front of the door.

"I need to talk to you about the washing business."

He lifted the cup to his lips then lowered it without taking a sip. "Okay. Do you need me to string additional lines?"

"Oh, no." She looked in the direction of the sod house. "We aren't taking enough washing in to fill the ones we have now."

"You're not wrong to refuse to work on credit, if that's what you're pondering. I do think your business will pick up once the railroad announces where the town will be built. More people will come and that will bring in cash."

Cora's trust-filled gaze met his. "I was thinking if bartering works out with Al, maybe it will work out with others, help us to fill up our larder so we can concentrate on proving up the homestead."

Pretty and smart. He admired Cora's determination to keep her home together, give her son roots and a place to grow. A boy needed a loving home. A childhood longing lassoed Luke's heart and squeezed his insides.

He turned from Cora and marched toward Dutch, trying to stomp life's disappointments back to the recesses of his memory. He set the cup on the wagon seat.

Soft warmth touched his back. "I'm sorry, Luke. I didn't mean to upset you. I value your opinion. You're such a good businessman."

Her words of praise stirred something in his soul. He turned. His eyes searched her face, roved her body. How could this sprite of a girl touch his soul in such a big way? He reached out with one arm and pulled her to him, lifting her slightly off the ground,

Her eyes widened with surprise and her lips began to form words that he didn't want to hear. He knew she was in mourning, but she was everything a good woman should be—loving, kind, gracious, a good mother...

All reasoning left his thoughts. Just a brush of her lips, a light taste of her sweetness was all he needed. He dipped his head, intending to graze her mouth briefly and gently. When their lips made contact, the welled-up emotion rushed from him.

The slight quiver of her lower lip coaxed him to quell its tremble with his own. He deepened the kiss.

Cora hummed low in her throat before her lips succumbed to his.

Luke strained to keep the kiss chaste. She was soft and warm and moved his heart. A long-ago feeling burst through him and filled him with happiness.

He yearned for acceptance. He yearned for happiness. He yearned for love.

Panic pushed out the bliss swirling through Luke's heart. *Love?*

## Chapter 7

"I beg your pardon, ma'am." Luke loosened his grip, eyes wide and frantic.

*Ma'am?* Cora lifted her fingers to her lips where Luke's warmth lingered. "What's wrong?" She drew her brows together in confusion. Had she offended him?

"Nothing. I was out of line. You're in mourning." Luke turned back to Dutch and fumbled with the harness. "Best go back into the house now until I have the wagon ready to go."

Cora pulled her shawl tighter. "Luke." Her voice heady from the intimacy they'd just shared.

"Go on now, Cora. You're a fine lady and it's not proper to be alone with a man in the barn."

Dutch snorted at her high-pitched gasp. The glee in her heart evaporated at Luke's terse words. Moisture sprang to her eyes. Stunned, she blinked back her tears and stared at the back of his work coat.

They'd kissed. A million questions ran through her mind. Questions she needed to have answered. What were his intentions? Were they courting? As she stared at his back, a different thought formed. "Why aren't you wearing your fine suit to church?"

The creaking of the wagon as Dutch shifted his weight was her only answer.

"Are you changing when we get to town?"

Luke's shoulders heaved with a deep breath. "Cora, go on inside and let me be."

Cora narrowed her eyes. Was he dismissing her after he'd made advances? Hot anger glowed inside her like the pine embers in the cookstove. "I will not be ordered to leave my own barn. Now answer my question."

The firmness in her voice spurred Luke to turn. He'd set his jaw. Coolness replaced the tenderness she'd witnessed in his brown eyes. His cold stare bored into her until she felt the chill deep in her soul. She clutched her shawl tighter.

"I don't go to church."

"But..."

He held up his hand. "There are no buts about it. Your God doesn't exist for me."

Luke's admission weighed heavy on Cora's heart, making the one-mile trip to the proposed town site seem endless.

Surprise registered on Luke's features when Bertha climbed up beside him on the bench seat. Relieved she could put distance between them, Cora eased into a comfortable position in the wagon box. She leaned against the wagon side, cradling Henry close.

In a short time she'd grown fond of Luke. Very fond of him. By his actions in the barn, she guessed he fancied her, too. Humiliation's blush burned her face at her weakness. Her Christian beliefs didn't allow her to yoke herself to an unbeliever.

How could a kiss that only lasted an instant turn her thoughts into a swirling turmoil? She lifted a fist to her mouth to stifle a moan, then rubbed her knuckles hard against her lips, hoping to erase the sensation of Luke's kiss. It didn't work. The soft, tender way he'd expressed his feelings still lingered.

Once they reached the edge of the camp area, Luke pulled the wagon to a hitching post Cora didn't remember seeing on her first visit to the makeshift town.

"My goodness!" Bertha exclaimed. "Look at all these people."

The wagon jiggled when Luke jumped from the driver's seat to hitch Dutch. He rounded the front of the wagon to help Bertha dismount. Cora handed Henry to Bertha over the side of the wagon before she scooted to the end of the buckboard.

Luke stood with his hand out, ready to help her out of the wagon. She slipped from the buckboard's box using the side to steady herself until both feet were firmly planted on the ground.

"I guess my services are no longer needed here. I'll see you after church."

"You aren't joining us, Luke?" The perplexed look on Bertha's face matched the emotions in Cora's heart.

"Not today, ma'am." Luke tipped his hat and walked in the opposite direction.

Surveying the area, Cora gathered the quilts they'd brought to sit on and started to walk alongside Bertha to the open stretch of land past the tents where others had gathered.

The short shoots of grass gave the land a velvety look. Several narrow rock formations jutted from the ground, creating a natural pulpit. The location was the perfect place to worship God's glory.

"Good morning, ladies."

Cora stopped in her tracks. Lost in her anger at Luke, she'd let her guard down, paid no attention to her surroundings.

"Clement." Bertha greeted their neighbor with her usual enthusiasm. "Isn't it grand to be able to attend a worship service?"

The swish of Bertha's twill skirt came closer to where Cora stood frozen to the ground.

"Why indeed it is." Clement's voice followed Bertha's rustle. "May I join you ladies on your rustic pews?"

He stopped beside Cora and held his hand out, motioning for her to give him the quilts bundled in her arms.

The bristly hairs of his moustache turned up. His smirk victorious, he'd won the right to sit beside them.

"It would only be fitting." Bertha gushed. "You can visit with Mr. Vernon. He plans to share our pew, too." Bertha craned her neck. "There's Al." She pointed, making sure Cora saw the direction she was headed.

Cora started to follow Bertha but Clement grabbed the edge of a quilt. Holding the quilts tight to her body, she leaned away from him.

"I didn't realize Al was sitting with us." Cora fixed an innocent look on her face and shrugged at Clement. "I didn't bring large enough quilts. I'm afraid there's no room for you."

Anger flashed in Clement's eyes. "I'm sure two quilts will seat four adults and a babe comfortably."

An icy shiver climbed up her spine. With no one else in the vicinity, Clement showed his true colors. Cora didn't miss the angry edge in his voice. The threatening tone made her reconsider the rude words on the tip of her tongue.

She'd repeat what she'd been telling him since September, she was in mourning, in a loud, firm tone, so the people around them could hear.

Cora squared her shoulders and met Clement's cold stare. She opened her mouth to speak when a circle of warmth rested on her back, stopping her words.

"I'm sure four people can sit comfortably on the quilts." Luke stepped close to Cora's side, his statement matter-of-fact. "But they won't seat five."

Luke took a step in the direction of the gathering congregation, lightly pushing on Cora's back until she began walking.

After a few steps, Cora chanced a look at Luke. She knitted her brow. He still wore his everyday clothes. "Thank you."

"You're welcome." Luke nodded greetings to several people, never turning his head in her direction.

"I thought you didn't attend church." Cora leaned toward Luke and whispered.

"I don't."

Baffled, Cora's jaw dropped. "I don't understand."

Luke stopped and grabbed her by the shoulders. "I said that to get you away from Clement. Once you get settled beside Bertha and Al, I'm going back to my tent." His brown eyes swam with his concern.

"Why don't you stay?" Her voice rose. A lady walking past looked them up and down.

"No." Luke's refusal was firm even in his hushed tone.

"I'll feel safer with you there." She hoped he'd respond to her pleading.

His gaze lifted to the horizon then returned to search her face, his eyes held a deep sadness. Luke set his jaw. "No. Now let's go. Al, Bertha and Henry are waiting."

This time Luke put his hand on her elbow and strode

across the grassland to the area where the others gathered. Cora almost had to run to keep up.

"Where's Clement?" Bertha scowled, tilting her head to look past Cora and Luke.

"He's not joining this group." Luke pulled the quilts from Cora's arms.

Handing one to Al, the men had them situated on the ground in minutes.

"Are you staying?" Al's cheery question didn't match the look that the men exchanged.

Luke shook his head and Al nodded his understanding.

True to his word, Luke left when the reverend hushed the congregation. Cora watched him walk off and kept her eyes on his back until he disappeared amidst the wagons. The Good Book said not to yoke yourself with unbelievers. Even though her heart felt differently, being a child of God she needed to obey His word.

Henry gurgled. She held her hands out to Bertha. She placed Henry vertically on her chest and rested his head on her shoulder. He'd need a man to look up to and teach him the golden rule. He needed a father with a solid relationship with God.

Cora sighed. Even though she'd only known Luke a matter of weeks, she had the silly notion he might be the man to provide those things for Henry. She lifted her eyes and caught sight of Clement, a man whose actions were contrary to the teachings of the Bible, yet here he was in church, acknowledging his Creator.

To her way of thinking, it should have been reversed. Luke showed honorable actions yet he didn't believe in God. Clement's character was despicable and he attended church every Sunday. Sadness settled in Cora's heart. She had no choice. She had to deny her feelings for Luke.

Cora bowed her head. *Dear Lord, give me strength.*

* * *

"We'll never get a potato crop." Bertha approached the porch where Cora sat in a straight-back chair, enjoying the mild May morning.

Setting a bucketful of water on the porch, Bertha put her hands on her lower back and stretched her overtaxed muscles. Her brown tweed skirt lifted a few inches in front, the hem tattered from years of wear.

Cora noticed Bertha staring at the garden spot behind the house as she walked from the well where she fetched the water.

"Everyone knows you have to plant them on Good Friday. The city slicker missed the date by two weeks."

The ache in Cora's heart intensified at the way Bertha mocked Luke, using a childish nickname after he'd done so much for them.

Without thinking, Cora jumped to his defense. "You should use his Christian..." Reconsidering her words, she stopped midsentence. Since last Sunday's service, she'd been trying hard to deny her feelings for him. She'd found childbirth easier to bear than refuting her growing feelings for Luke. The pain of delivering a baby, temporary and fleeting, was less severe than an aching heart.

Keeping her eyes fixed on her mending, she worked the needle in and out, securing a button to the cuff of a railroad worker's shirt. Looping the thread to tie off her stiches, she held it taunt and bit it, snapping the thread from the cotton. "Time will tell. It's nice having a big garden, a chance to fill our pantry."

"We wouldn't have to worry about our pantry if you'd allow a suitor."

Cora's head jerked up. The same old hope shone on Bertha's face, expecting this time Cora would consider her mourning period over and agree to court Clement. "I'm still in mourning. I'm honoring your son, Henry's father and my husband's memory."

A thread of guilt looped through her and knotted her stomach. Maybe that was why her heart and head spun with such turmoil. It was punishment for considering another so soon after her husband's passing. Freely kissing Luke like a wanton woman. Shame pricked her heart.

She needed to focus on her family's needs, not her own. She surveyed the farmyard. A chicken coop edged one side of the barn. Straight furrows, peppered with seed potatoes and root vegetable seeds, striped the land on the opposite side. They were waiting for the ground to warm to sow the more fragile seeds.

At least this would be considered an improvement to the land, since they couldn't afford the lumber or labor to construct a barn on the rock foundation they'd laid close to the crags last summer.

Squinting, Cora shielded her eyes from the morning sunshine. In the distance a puff of dirt swirled in the air.

"Someone's coming." Cora stood; her forgotten mending fell from her faded blue skirt to the porch floor. She strained to see if it were friend or foe.

The dappled-gray stallion galloped into the yard.

"Whoa." Luke dismounted before the horse came to a stop. Dropping his reins to the ground, he leaped onto the porch. Water from Bertha's bucket sloshed over the edge of the wooden pail from the shift in the porch boards.

"The railroad made their announcement today. They are building where the camp is—well, not exactly where the camp is, over a ways. My point is we are in the right spot to witness the birth of a town."

In Luke's excitement, his words came fast. He picked Cora up and swung her around. The heels of her boots bumped the legs of her chair. The chair teetered, its legs clicking on the porch floor.

Bertha scowled and looked as if she were about to comment on his inappropriate actions, but Luke continued talking to Cora.

"All my dreams are coming true and yours will, too. There is no doubt in my mind your laundry business will be a success."

Cora caught Luke's infectious enthusiasm and giggled.

"None of this has been for naught." He set Cora down and spread his arms wide.

Dizziness swayed Cora's movements, but she managed to catch Bertha in a hug. "In a very short time, this place will be ours. Our home. And no one can take it away from us."

The smile on Bertha's face was genuine, though it lacked enthusiasm.

"Don't you see? Hank's dream to own his own farm, maybe expand it into a ranch, will come true." Cora squeezed Bertha's shoulder, hoping to widen her smile.

"We still have a lot of work ahead of us before September. We've got one more crop to put in." Bertha nodded toward the sod house. The field Hank plotted hadn't been touched since last fall's harvest. The soil had settled in lumpy mounds over the winter and now waited for the turn of the plow.

The sowing of the field had slipped Cora's mind. What little money she'd squirreled away from the washings would need to be used for seed. Responsibility's weight wrung through her, twisting out all her excitement before hanging her out to dry.

Her certainty in proving up their homestead was fading. Two women couldn't get all the necessary work done. Unfortunately, they'd let tending their flock slide. Every

time Cora counted the sheep it seemed another was missing, lost to predators.

"You finally see what we're up against." Bertha's eyes
conveyed understanding. "There is a way to ease our burdens. Say the word and Clement will send a man to plow
our field."

Cora bit her lip and shook her head. She'd lose the homestead before agreeing to become Clement's wife.

"No." Luke jumped back up onto the porch.

Luke coming to her defense rallied Cora's spirit and
lifted her heart.

"I don't see how any of this is your business, Luke."
The unhappiness Bertha carried in her heart deepened the
angry lines in her features.

"I won't marry Clement." Cora placed her hand on Bertha's arm and looked her square in the eyes. "Ever."

Bertha huffed and marched into the house, letting the
door bang. Cora waited to hear Henry's wail from being
awakened from his nap. When no indication came that her
son was in distress, she turned to Luke.

"I'm sorry I rub her the wrong way," he said. "It's not
the first time. I guess it's my nature to affect people in a
negative way." Luke's face held a perplexed, faraway look.

Cora's breath heaved from her. Her eyes darted to the
house, then she stepped off the porch. Luke followed. When
they reached the iron pump, Cora turned to Luke. "Bertha
is just sad and scared. Her faith is low. She doesn't believe
a woman can nor should run a farm on her own."

Silence surrounded them. Did Luke agree with Bertha?

They walked toward the back of the sod house, stopping
by the edge of the field. Luke's nearness warmed her inside
and outside. She searched his profile while he surveyed the
field plot. The planes of his face, round and smooth, held a

schoolboy charm. She guessed he wore his moustache to give his baby face a mature appearance.

"You think with Bertha's help you can work the land."

It was hard to tell if Luke's words were a question or a statement. Cora laughed. "Call me crazy. I believe we can. Even though what lies before me—" Cora waved her hand toward the field "—is three hard days behind a plow. Bertha can keep up with the washing and ironing. Henry will be safe sitting in a basket in the shade while we work. It will be hard, but not impossible. This is my home and I intend to fight for it."

Luke clasped her hand, he wiggled his fingers until hers were interwoven in his. "I am in awe of your determination."

The spring sun's warmth was no match for the fiery blush creeping onto her cheeks from Luke's kind words and knowing he thought highly of her. Her heartbeat quickened, all thoughts of fighting her feelings for him thrown out like dirty wash water.

She turned to him, hoping the happiness she felt was reflected in her eyes in the same way pleasure danced in his. "Are people at the campsite celebrating?"

"Yes, everyone is firming up their building plans."

"Does the town have a name?"

Luke snorted then pursed his lips. "Yes, it's named after one of the railroad officials' daughters."

"Do you find it odd a father would want to honor his child?" Cora knitted her brows. Surely, Luke understood those feelings. She saw the way he looked at Henry.

A darkness veiled Luke's brown eyes. "It's not that." He looked across the terrain, lonesomeness settled on his face. His gazed returned to hers. "The town's name is Faith."

# Chapter 8

Every muscle in her body protested, throbbing with her every movement. The last thing she wanted to do was walk to town with Bertha to deliver their customers' washing and ironing. Dutch had worked so hard the past three days pulling the plow through the stubborn soil she couldn't hitch him to the wagon. He needed a rest. But she couldn't let Bertha know how strained she felt from plowing. She bit the edge of her lip to stifle a groan.

"Well, don't that beat all?" Bertha stopped walking and set the basket she carried on the ground. Cora stood beside her, jiggling Henry on her hip.

The tent and wagon city had shifted, leaving brown patches of dirt and matted grass for the railroad to build over. The open area where the reverend held church services was no longer visible.

"Faith, South Dakota. It's a fitting name, don't you think?" Cora looked at Bertha.

She nodded her head. "All these people saw a new beginning, a new life even before it was here."

"The same way we did when we left our Eastern home." Cora patted Bertha's back and received a wry look.

"Maybe you and Hank had faith in that decision. And you still do." Bertha sighed. She bent and picked up the basket. "Where do you suppose we'll find Al and Luke?"

Cora gingerly shrugged, shifted Henry to the other side of her body and began to walk on the main path through the canvas city. At the far end of the street men were putting up the framework for walls.

Bertha fell into step. "Do you think the large building is the terminus?"

Before Cora could speculate on the business at the end of the street, she spotted Luke and Al standing in a group of men, who also seemed interested in the building going up.

When they saw the women, they left the group and walked toward them.

"How is my big boy?" Luke scooped Henry from Cora's arms, giving her aching muscles a much-needed reprieve.

Henry waved his chubby fist in the air and cooed. Luke waggled his finger and Henry smiled. Cora's heart swelled at the bond between her son and Luke.

She caught her breath. *Lord, these are the times I need Your help.* It was so hard not to act on her feelings for Luke. Yet it was the thing she had to do.

"Let me unburden you." Al took the basket from Bertha's arms.

"What you think, ladies?" Luke pointed to an area nearby. "We squatted on a prime location. We'll be a block away from the depot if we're the highest bidders when the land goes to auction in July."

Cora clapped her hands. "Wonderful. Al, is your barbershop beside Luke's hotel?"

"I'm afraid not." Al's expression turned sour. "I can't afford my own land and the building materials, too."

"What?" Bertha took a step closer to Al and laid her hand on his forearm.

Luke's jaw set and his brown eyes darkened. He nodded toward the building being erected. "Clement's building a lumberyard on the edge of his property. Somehow he's managed to purchase all the available lumber in the area. He's doubled the price of the wood he's not using to build his own business."

"Luke and I had to partner up in order to afford to buy land and build. My barbershop will be in the hotel."

"Hmm..." Bertha made a throaty sound that showed her surprise.

Cora wondered if this would make Bertha see that Clement only pretended to be upstanding.

"Perhaps that will work out better." Cora's offer of hope made Al smile.

"Perhaps it will. Bertha, shall I accompany you while you deliver the laundry? Since the town has shifted, I can help you find your customers." Al lifted the basket.

"I'd be obliged if you did." Bertha turned to Cora. "Have Luke show you where to buy the seeds for the field. Al and I will meet you back here."

Cora nodded, stifling a giggle. Al, carrying the basket with both hands, managed to offer the crook of his elbow to Bertha.

"Let me show you our fine establishment." Luke pulled a piece of paper from his pocket and walked toward his tent. Cora followed behind.

Luke handed Cora the paper to hold while he jiggled Henry, even though the baby seemed content peering over Luke's shoulder.

"This will be the dining room." Luke motioned with

his finger. "A small kitchen and my quarters will be off the back."

Cora nodded, her head following the path Luke's finger traced on his building plans.

"This is where the front desk will be." Luke tapped the opposite side of the paper. "The staircase will be right beside it. We have room for a small lobby. My plan was to have a large lobby where guests could visit. Now Al's barbershop will fill most of the space. All the sleeping rooms are upstairs."

"You have quite a plan. How many rooms will be upstairs?" Cora followed Luke's skyward gaze.

Narrow-eyed, he calculated the space. "I think six—two large rooms to house families or traveling companions, four smaller individual rooms."

"This is quite an undertaking. Where will Al sleep?"

Luke scratched his chin. "I've offered to let him bunk in my room. He insists the area isn't even big enough for me. He thinks a small bed will fit under the staircase and he will sleep there."

"That's pretty tight quarters." Cora frowned. "For both of you."

"It is. We both had to adjust our plans. We'll have to make do until our businesses take off."

"I suppose it's better than sleeping in a tent. I know the sod house was better than sleeping in the wagon or on the ground." Cora tried to find a silver lining in this change of plans for both Al and Luke.

Luke's jaw set. "It's not a very neighborly thing Clement is doing, charging double for lumber."

Henry let out a high-pitched coo and shook his fist.

A hearty laugh bounced out of Luke. "I'm glad you agree with me, Henry." He stretched his arms high in the air and wiggled Henry back and forth.

Pure joy shined from Henry and Luke's faces. A strong feeling anchored itself inside Cora. In such a short time, Luke had become a special addition to their lives, yet all he'd ever be was a friend. Her heart squeezed tight in disagreement with her thoughts. She bit the corner of her lip.

"What?" Luke's smile faded. "Am I being too rough with your son?" Luke pulled Henry into the crook of his arm.

Swallowing hard, Cora smiled. "No, that's not it at all. Besides..." Cora stepped closer to Luke and cupped Henry's head in her hands, planting a kiss on his forehead. "Boys need to roughhouse."

When she lifted her eyes, tenderness etched Luke's features. His brown eyes gleamed with happiness and love. Her breath caught in her chest when he lowered his head in the same way he had in the barn.

Her whole being wanted to lean into him, accept his affection, but her belief in God's teaching was strong. Straightening her spine and her resolve, she leaned away from him.

In an instant, the light shining from his eyes dimmed. Hurt pinched his handsome features.

"I think you'd better show me where I can buy the seed for my field."

The nervous tap of Cora's foot on the ground jiggled her body. She craned her neck one way and then the other, trying to catch sight of Bertha and Al.

It was apparent to Luke she didn't want to be alone with him. Why would she? Every time they were together he made advances that only a suitor should.

His deep exhale startled Henry. His little body jerked then relaxed against Luke's arm, where he dozed.

When Luke was around Cora, she stirred strong feelings and made the urge to be part of a loving family, something he'd longed for his whole life, seem possible. That's how it felt today. She showed interest when he described his hotel, when he played with Henry, and when he tried to give her a kiss.

Until the instant when their lips almost touched. Confusion furrowed Luke's brow. She'd accepted his kiss the first time in the barn, even responded to it. The only thing different today was the location and Henry presence.

Her foot wiggling stopped. She rose to her tiptoes still craning her neck.

"They'll be along soon."

His words of comfort were rewarded with only a brief glance. He released another deep sigh, more careful than the first so he didn't disturb Henry.

Even in her agitated state, Cora was beautiful, maybe more so. She wore a pink cotton skirt with a matching straw hat. A sprig of white daisies adorned the right side of her hat brim.

The rosy color on her cheeks, a shade or two darker than the hat framing her face, created an appealing glow. Her white blouse had lace cuffs halfway up her arm. The same lace covered the bodice of the garment reaching up to ensconce her neck. The fashion was dated, but she looked timeless.

When the general store was fully stocked Luke intended to buy her a fashionable dress. His heart dropped. A longing to buy a woman gifts was something only a betrothed or married man should feel, yet he daydreamed of the things he wanted to buy Cora and Henry to make their life easier and better. Besides he couldn't purchase anything extra until the hotel turned a profit. Clement's outrageous prices for building materials would take most of his savings.

"There they are!"

Al and Bertha approached the same way they'd left, Al

holding a full basket, Bertha's hand secure in the crook of Al's arm. They visited while they strolled, not even noticing Cora's frantic waving. Bertha's animated face gave her a youthful appearance.

"Couldn't you find all the folks to make deliveries to?" Cora sounded disappointed.

"Oh, we found them. These are new customers. The rusty water in these parts is turning their clothes red. Even adding bluing to the water isn't helping." Bertha pulled an article of clothing from a feed sack. Red water marks ran through a tan work shirt, giving it a ghastly hue.

"I don't know if we can get this stain out." Cora ran her hands over the shirt, inspecting both sides of the fabric.

Bertha held up her hands. "I didn't make any promises, other than we'd do our best."

Cora nodded at Bertha. "We need to settle up." She cocked her head toward a wagon that served as the general store while the building was being erected.

Al set the basket on the ground and watched the women walk away. "Those are two of the finest woman I've ever met."

Luke smiled and nodded.

"Bertha has a lovely soul and is a pleasure to spend time with."

It took all of Luke's effort to keep his eyes from narrowing and ask if they were talking about the same woman.

Al didn't even notice Luke's change of expression as his eyes followed Bertha's every movement. "I want to ask her for courting privileges, although I don't have much to offer her right now."

He pulled his gaze from the two women finalizing their order and met Luke's stare. "Have you asked Cora about courting? It appears you're ready to settle down." Al nodded at Henry snoozing in Luke's arms.

Looking down at Henry so chubby and cute, Luke's heart filled with happiness. He'd considered the prospect of courting Cora from every angle a man could, but it all came back to his childhood. He'd experienced family life and wanted no part of it. All of this idle time was making him lose his focus. He needed to build a profitable business, not a family.

He grazed Henry's cheek with his knuckle and looked up at Al. In the few weeks he'd known Al, he'd grown to trust him. Al was different from most men of his generation. He didn't try to force his strong opinions on others. Unlike Clement and Luke's father, Al allowed others to express ideas different from his own.

"I have." Luke nodded his head. "I don't know that I'm ready to settle down. Besides, I'm in a fix, too. I only have dreams to offer. As a matter of fact—" Luke rubbed his moustache with his index finger "—she probably has more to offer than I do. A homestead with only a few months left to prove up and good water." He wrinkled his brow and looked in the direction where the lumberyard was being built.

"Don't let it stop you. You are on your way to being a business owner." Al clapped him on the back.

Al's encouragement was lost on Luke. His thoughts had turned to the suspicions he had about Clement. "I saw something..."

"Where?" Luke turned and saw Cora standing a few feet away. Lost in thought, Luke hadn't been aware that the women had returned. Bertha and Al had stepped away and were engrossed in a private whispered conversation.

"Well." Luke cleared his throat. It wasn't a secret he wanted to keep from her, but he didn't want to upset her. That floating light troubled his mind, yet he didn't know for sure if he'd even seen something. Until he did, he'd keep the information to himself. "I was going to ask Al a question, but I see he's already engaged in a conversation."

Cora giggled. "I haven't seen Bertha this happy in a long time. Al is such a blessing to her, an answer to my prayer for her happiness."

Luke's spine stiffened. A bitter retort burned on his lips. He pursed them tight. He knew firsthand God didn't answer prayers. How could he convince Cora of that truth?

Her look of contentment when she turned her attention back to Luke dissolved his urge to make his case about God.

She lifted the basket filled with soiled clothes. "I was worried our business might not take off. This is encouraging. I want to put some fixtures in the sod house, making it our permanent washroom."

"Isn't it your permanent washroom now?" Luke switched Henry to his other arm.

"Yes. But I need to figure out a way to heat the water in the sod house. Right now, we carry it from the pump to the cookstove only to carry it out to the soddy. It'd save us time if we could do all the work in one place. The grass roof is still in good condition and doesn't leak. The sod house stays cool during the warm summer days. We'd store folks' clothes in there until they are picked up or we deliver. After all, if the garden produces in abundance, we'll need the shelving we use in the pantry to store our canned goods."

They had plenty of empty space on their pantry shelves, but Luke appreciated Cora's ambition and faith that everything would work. *And faith?* Never in his life had he admired anyone for having faith. He pulled his lips into a frown.

"So?" Cora looked at him in an exasperated way.

He raised his eyebrows in question.

Cora sighed deeply. "You don't think it's a good idea. I can tell by your frown."

"It is a fine idea. What did you use to heat the sod house? A fireplace?"

"No, the cookstove."

Luke rubbed his chin with his hand. "You have a large cookstove. It must have taken up most of the space in the soddy before you moved it into the house."

Cora nodded. "A small potbellied stove would work perfectly, but..."

Her sentence trailed off and Luke knew why. There wasn't any money to purchase a small stove. "You could make a fire pit outside. There are more than enough rocks on your property to make a ring around it to keep the fire from spreading."

"True. We still wouldn't be able to heat our iron, though." Exasperation sounded in Cora's sigh, yet determination flickered in her eyes.

Luke knew she was pondering a way to make this work. He delighted at the pretty way she pursed her lips and narrowed her eyes in contemplation.

"Why, yes, she is here. She's right over there."

Luke and Cora turned. Striding toward them were Bertha, Clement and Al. Al lagged behind, shaking his head, an indication to Luke he'd tried to stop this meeting and failed. Al shared Luke's dislike of Clement.

Cora turned to Luke. Frightened eyes searched his face. He resisted the urge to pull her to him.

"I was wondering if you'd care for a tour of my building." Clement extended his hand to Cora.

"We haven't the time." Cora kept her hands stuck in the pockets of her skirt. "We must be getting home before sundown."

"It will only take a minute."

"No." The force in Cora's one word woke Henry, who grunted in discomfort.

Clement's face creased with anger.

Henry didn't take well to being awakened and his full-fledged cry echoed through the tent town. Cora took him from Luke's arms and bounced him, which did little to comfort him or soothe his cries.

"Cora, where are your manners?" Bertha chided, shouting over Henry's wails. "An intended should be interested in her man's projects."

"He is not my intended." Cora shot a look at Bertha. "It's time for us to head home."

Clement looked around. "I don't see your wagon. Perhaps you'd allow me to escort you home in my buggy."

Luke saw the threat in his hungry eyes, even though Clement's words and tone were polite so anyone within earshot wouldn't suspect he was up to no good.

"No, thank you." Cora shouted over Henry's crying. "We can manage."

"How are we going to carry everything?" Bertha crossed her arms. Her sour expression replaced the happiness that had so recently shone on her face. "We didn't plan on bringing home more washing."

A wide, smug smile spread across Clement's face. He didn't think Cora had an answer for her mother-in-law.

Luke waited. Cora didn't utter a word of rebuttal. She held Henry tighter and jostled him more.

"It's settled then." Clement's voice dripped with victory.

Henry's cries rose in pitch.

"Not so fast." Luke stepped in between Clement and Cora. "I already offered to help tote the ladies' supplies home. Right, Cora?"

Cora peeked around Luke. "Why, yes, you did. So you see, even though it was neighborly of you, Clement, we don't need your services."

Clement glowered at Luke and Henry stopped crying.

# Chapter 9

Cora watched Clement stalk away. The erratic beat of her heart started to slow.

"I'll go with Bertha to get their supplies from the store." Al offered Bertha his arm.

"Thank you." Cora looked at Luke, who didn't meet her eyes. He kept his disgust-filled gaze on Clement's back.

"You need to have a talk with your mother-in-law."

Instantly, Cora lowered her head. The powdery dirt kicked up by many boots on the makeshift street was a reminder of how Clement made her feel that spring day by the rocky crags of her property. She closed her eyes, but the shameful feeling remained.

She nodded, knowing that Luke was right. She needed to tell Bertha what Clement had tried the day she was gathering fertilizer for their garden.

Fear kindled a flame in the pit of her stomach and stoked the pace of her heart. Would Bertha think she encouraged

Clement's actions? Or, worse, insist the event sealed a marriage vow? Fiery heat licked up her neck and settled on her cheeks at the thought of such an appalling conversation.

"Cora, I didn't mean to upset you."

Lifting her head and opening her eyes, Cora searched Luke's face.

He reached out. His rough knuckles brushed against her burning cheek, his eyes reflected his concern. "She needs to know sooner rather than later."

Managing a weak smile, Cora nodded. She'd muster the strength to broach the subject.

In minutes, Al and Bertha returned with a box of supplies and a sack of seed. Luke picked up the heaping basket of laundry and in silence he led the way out of town.

Cora followed, making sure to keep behind him even though she longed to walk by his side, not just today, but the rest of her life.

She gave her head a small shake, trying to remove such nonsense from her thoughts. Luke was a perfect match for her in almost in every way. Sadness saturated her like soapy, water-soaked cloth. Why wasn't he a Christian?

"My arms ache."

Cora turned.

Bertha had stopped walking and put down the box of supplies she carried.

"Let's trade." Cora turned and held Henry at arm's length.

Every muscle in Cora's body throbbed from the time spent behind the plow, but she'd ease Bertha's burden if she could.

"Why, we should have thought of that in the first place." Al stood beside Bertha with a sack of seed thrown over his shoulder. "The ladies should be carrying the lightest load."

Luke turned and retraced his steps.

Cora pulled Henry back to her bosom when Bertha made no motion to take him.

"No, we should have been riding in the comfort of a buggy." Bertha crossed her arms and narrowed her eyes at Cora. "And you men could be doing whatever you planned to do today." She nodded her head so hard her hat slid forward then back and teetered for a few seconds.

A deep scowl formed on Luke's handsome face. He set the basket on the ground, and his hands curled into fists. Cora recognized the gesture as a show of his anger. She'd never witnessed him throwing a punch, and was certain he wouldn't hit a woman, yet she was glad she stood between them so she could deflect their anger.

Luke worked his jaw back and forth. Was he fighting to hold back his words?

"Now, Bertha, it's up to Cora to decide who she wants for a suitor, not you." Al's soft voice, silky smooth, cut through the tension.

Bertha snorted. "I'm her elder."

For the first time since meeting Al, Bertha's eyes didn't twinkle when she looked at him.

"Bertha, in matters of the heart, a person has to make their own decisions." Al laid his hand on Bertha's arm.

Surprise widened Cora's eyes when Bertha's lip trembled.

"Clement makes a good suitor. He has an established ranch. He can break any horse, and he's a fine, churchgoing man." Bertha's eyes, dulled with anger, looked Luke up and down.

Her words echoed through Cora's heart. Every Sunday, Luke would pick them up for church, drop them off and disappear before the worship service began.

Al interrupted Cora's thoughts. "Clement might make

a good suitor for a woman at least forty years older than Cora."

Al's words changed Bertha's expression to a look of consideration. Had she never calculated their age difference?

"Cora's a young woman on the brink of life. My guess is Clement's close to the sixth decade of his. Besides, I don't know if I'd describe Clement as a fine man. He's putting quite a few of us in a bind with those lumber prices."

Bertha lowered her chin and eyes. "You're right, Al," she whispered. "I won't bother Cora anymore about allowing Clement to court her."

Al chucked her chin until she lifted it and gave him a slight smile. He kissed the tip of her nose then straightened her hat.

A grunt of astonishment sounded over Cora's shoulder. She turned. Luke raised his eyebrows and whispered, "Well, I'll be."

Cora raised and lowered the iron pump's handle until water gushed from the spout.

The July sun burned strong and hot. Quiet no longer surrounded their homestead. The summer breeze lifted the music of progress and swept it across the plains to echo off the rocky bluff. The clang of iron rang through the air with each new piece of track laid across the prairie. The steady drum of railroad workers' hammers, erecting the terminus and depot a short mile away, made the promise of a new town a reality.

She lifted the enamel dipper they'd hooked to the bucket and ran it through the water. Bringing the cool, clear well water to her lips, Cora refreshed her body after hanging the last of the washing on the line. She replaced the dipper on the bucket, took her large straw hat off and wiped her brow with the back of her arm.

In a few days, they'd celebrate the Fourth of July. After the Independence Day holiday, the railroad would auction the town's land then private citizens' hammers would add to the town's heartbeat, including Luke and Al's.

Between the four of them, the homestead had shaped up. They'd mended the fence and penned the remaining sheep; so far, they hadn't lost anymore and by Cora's calculations actually had three more head since spring's birthing season.

"Henry is down for a nap." Bertha stepped off the porch, adjusting Hank's old wide-brimmed hat on her head. "We should have time to get the potato garden hoed."

A smile tugged at Cora's lips. Bertha had found a new energy and attitude since Al asked to be her suitor. He instilled her with hope in the future. Cora understood. Everything seemed possible when you were in love.

The twist of Cora's heart pursed her lips. She was happy Bertha had found a good, God-fearing man. She wished she could say the same thing. Although she missed Hank, it was time for her to move on, too. She wished it could be with Luke. He had every good quality a woman could hope for, except one.

She sighed and lifted another dipper of water to her lips, took a sip and offered it to Bertha.

The wind snapped the cotton clothing hanging to dry. All three clotheslines were filled two times a week. Significant rain and sun nurtured the plants and weeds in the garden. Her sorghum crop was coming in nicely. Although it was a little early to count her blessings, she was anyway. The fear that she'd lose another farm had plagued her since Hank's death. When her father had died, the bank owned more of her father's land than he had, and through no fault of her own she was left without a home. Now that trepidation was little more than a memory. She'd prove up her homestead, keep her family together and never be homeless again.

A bridle's jingle pulled Cora from her thoughts. Neither Luke nor Al said they'd be out at the homestead this afternoon, but these days they received many visitors bringing their laundry to the homestead.

Cora turned around with a bright smile in place ready to greet a customer. Her smile immediately faded.

"Good afternoon, ladies." Clement tugged the reins hard to stop his horse.

"Clement." Bertha nodded her greeting. "I delivered your wash yesterday. I left it with the hired hand and received our pay."

"I know." Clement nodded. "I thought I'd drop by and see how my neighbors are doing." With effort he dismounted, letting his reins drop to the ground. "Mind if I have a drink of your cold well water?"

"Help yourself." Cora took two large steps away from the iron pump.

Clement drank two dippers full of water from the bucket. "Ah, your water is so good. It helps you out with the laundry business, too. Look at those whites." Clement tipped his head toward the clothesline.

Cora frowned, watching Clement make a circle around the well while surveying their farmyard. "You've made quite a few improvements since last year."

He lifted a finger. "Chicken coop."

A second finger stood erect. "Two gardens. Your required crop. A laundry business. Your herd penned instead of running wild." With each item listed, Clement raised a digit until he held one palm up in the air, pudgy fingers outstretched. "Quite impressive for two women."

"Well, we've had some..."

"God has certainly blessed us." Cora cut Bertha off.

Clement knew Luke and Al helped them, which wasn't against the rules.

"Why, yes, He has." Clement turned a beady-eyed stare on Cora. "Not everyone has been so lucky. Even with the railroad coming and the promise of a town, your neighbors to the south had to sell, lost their cattle."

"What? Mr. Hanson had the best fences in these parts." Bertha turned a shocked face to Cora.

"Yes, he did." Suspicion colored Cora's words. She took small steps closer to the pump where Bertha rested the hoes.

Clement cocked an eyebrow and looked from Bertha to Cora. "They didn't run away. Must have got a disease. Found them all dead."

Bertha gasped.

Cora held Clement's icy stare. "From what?"

"Don't know." Clement shrugged, jiggling his entire body. "Hoof and mouth. Maybe they drank some tainted water." Clement lifted himself up on his tiptoes and craned his neck. "How are those sheep of yours doing? I haven't seen them feeding by the rocks lately."

He turned his gaze to Cora and winked.

Panic punched the air from her lungs. Her gasp echoed around the farmyard. She lowered her eyes. She remembered what Luke told her. She couldn't let Clement see her fear. It gave him the advantage. She gritted her teeth in an attempt to steel her resolve. *Dear Lord, give me strength.*

Peace replaced her terror. She lifted her head, intending to tell him the whereabouts of their livestock was none of his business.

"Fine," Bertha said. "They're just over the slight knoll behind the soddy in our grassy land. Luke and Al helped us fix the fence and round them up so we could keep them closer to the house. We had quite a few go missing over the winter."

Cora cringed. Bertha needed to stop feeding Clement information. It was clear that's why he'd stopped by today. He wanted to size up their homestead, make note of their improvements. Cora didn't like it one bit. He hated sheep and she was certain he wasn't interested in her herd's well-being.

"You did." Clement pulled on the end of his moustache. "Disease?"

"Predators."

Clement didn't miss the insult in Cora's words. He turned. His eyes alight with arrogance, a haughty smile wrinkled his face.

Even though fear shook Cora's insides, she set her jaw in the same way Luke did to keep Clement from seeing her fear. She prayed her voice wouldn't give her away by shaking. "Did you buy out the Hanson's?"

"Why, yes, I did." Clement slowly walked toward Cora. She tightened her grip on the hoe handle.

"It was the Christian thing to do. I couldn't let them starve."

"What are they going to do?" Bertha asked.

Out of the corner of her eye, Cora saw Bertha move toward the other hoe. Did she finally see Clement for the scoundrel that he was? Clement never turned to address Bertha. He kept his unnerving gaze on Cora.

"They're planning on heading back East." Clement stepped closer to Cora. "It would behoove you to grant me suitor privileges. I'm well on my way to being a land baron and a pioneer of the community of Faith."

Her snort was involuntary. "The railroad is pioneering the town, not you. I've told you many times. I'm in mourning and not accepting suitors." Cora's words hissed through her clenched teeth. "Get off my homestead."

Clement turned to Bertha. "Haven't you talked some

sense into her yet? You'd have a comfortable life, no more washing and hoeing. A pillar of the community with the same life of leisure you had in the East."

His tone changed to a smooth, soothing lilt, playing on Bertha's longings. Cora's breath became ragged. Her pulse resounded in her ears. Would Bertha keep her promise to Al?

"She's honoring my son's memory the way the Lord intends. Besides, Clement, she is a little young for you." Bertha held the hoe handle with both hands, giving the appearance she cowered behind it.

Clement's portly frame seemed to expand with the deep breath he took. He turned, his eyes filled with threat. "You will regret the day you ordered me from your property."

"I will not. Now, if you've had your fill of our well water, please leave. We have work to do."

Clement stalked to his horse and mounted him in one quick movement. He rode close to where she stood, too close.

Her legs felt so weak she thought she would crumple to the ground. She pushed hard on the hoe handle, using it for support. He leaned over his saddle, eyes filled with hate. "You will become my wife," he said quietly so only she could hear. "The next time I catch you alone, you will be mine." His evil laugh surrounded her, drowning out all other sounds. He turned his horse and galloped off.

Shudders overtook her. She'd been up to the task of proving up her homestead under the regulations set by the government. She didn't know if she could protect it and herself from Clement.

"Cora, are you all right?" Bertha wrapped an arm around her shoulders. "You're white as Al's towels on the clothesline. What did he say to you?"

The squawk of chickens and the flap of wings against

wire broke Cora out of her stupor. Her eyes focused on the puffs of dirt Luke's and Al's horses hooves stirred up beside the chicken coop.

"When did they get here?" She searched Bertha's concern-filled face.

"They just rode in. Didn't you hear the horses?" Bertha held a dipper of water to Cora's lips.

The cool liquid shocked her back into awareness. Giving her head a shake, she realized the hoe still held the brunt of her weight.

"Are you two all right?" Luke dismounted and jogged toward the two women.

"We were out hunting when we saw Clement riding out of here like a posse was chasing him." Al joined the group standing beside Bertha.

"I am. Clement gave Cora quite a scare." Bertha offered the dipper of water she held to Al.

"Cora." Luke grabbed her shoulders and leaned down to look her in the eyes. "Did he hurt you?"

"No." She shook her head. "He threatened me. He said next time he found me alone, I wouldn't be so lucky."

Horror crossed over Luke's features before he set his jaw. He drew Cora into a tight embrace. "That isn't going to happen. I won't let it."

Cora melded into the safety and warmth of Luke's arms. His nearness eased her fears, restored her hope.

"What did he mean?" Bertha walked closer to Cora and Luke.

Luke's strong arms loosened around Cora. "You haven't told her."

Moisture threatened Cora's eyes. She bit at her upper lip, shaking her head.

"Tell her." The directness in Luke's voice indicated she couldn't put off this uncomfortable conversation any longer.

She hung her head. "One day this spring, while I was in the rocky crags with the sheep, Clement tried to take advantage of me." Hearing the words ring out through the air, she felt stronger. She lifted her eyes to meet Bertha's and expected to find her scolding stare.

Instead Berth's momentary shock was replaced with anger.

"Did he?" Bertha walked up to her and clasped her hand. The rough calluses from the iron familiar and comforting. "Did he..." Bertha's whisper trailed off before all of the words could come.

"No. Luke came to find me in the nick of time."

Bertha pulled her into a hug. "He had me fooled. He isn't a fine man. I'm so sorry I've pressured you into allowing him to court you. Please forgive me?"

The brief hug restored her faith in her mother-in-law's support. "I do."

The incident no longer made her feel ashamed. She'd done nothing wrong. She looked at Al, whose normal jovial expression showed his disgust. When she turned to Luke, his contempt for Clement was evident on his face.

"Why was he here anyway?" Luke paced around the pump. "Didn't you deliver his laundry yesterday?"

Bertha nodded.

"I think." Cora frowned, trying to push the fuzz of shock from her mind.

"He wanted to tell us our neighbor, Mr. Hanson, lost his homestead." Bertha inserted when Cora paused.

"Yes." Cora looked at Luke, who stopped pacing. "And I think he was checking out the state of our homestead. He wasn't happy with all of the improvements. I don't think it's me he really wants. I think it's my land."

Luke and Al exchanged a knowing nod.

"I don't know what to do." Cora wrung her hands.

"I do." Luke stepped up to her and took off his hat. He ran his long fingers through the loose waves. "Cora, would you allow me courting privileges?"

Cora's eyes went wide. *Yes!* Her heart screamed its answer, but she shook her head. "I can't."

The pleading expression on Luke's face twisted her heart.

"I know you are in mourning, but..."

"It's not because I'm mourning." Hot tears burned her eyes. More than anything she wanted to throw her arms around his neck and scream, "Yes!" yet she couldn't. Regret clogged her throat. She swallowed hard. "I can't be yoked with a nonbeliever."

Luke's face pinched with confusion.

"You." Cora laid her hand on Luke's arm. "Are not a Christian."

# Chapter 10

"Are you still champing at the bit about Cora's refusal?" Al sat on an apple crate balancing his speckled blue tin mug on his knee.

"No." Luke glowered at his friend and stalked back and forth in front of his tent. Although that was exactly what he was doing and he didn't know why. He didn't think he would make a good family man, and yet he'd asked Cora's permission to court her! Didn't courting mean a man was seriously considering marriage? A part of him said that wasn't what he wanted, yet, he couldn't let Cora or Henry or even Bertha become prey to Clement's evil.

He looked up and surveyed his surroundings.

The town had come to life. The fifty or so people who'd set up makeshift homes in the last few months were lost in the throng of at least 150 folks bustling around.

"Where did all these people come from?" Luke almost snarled the question.

"Some are railroad workers. Some are cowboys with the rodeo." Al shrugged. "I'm sure some are curious to see the terminus. He rubbed his chin. "It's good for my business, though."

Luke snorted. "I wish the railroad would have auctioned off land in June. I'd have at least a room or two to rent. This isn't helping my business."

"Sit down before you wear out your boots, partner." Al motioned toward another crate. "It's filling my coffers, which is what we need to make sure we get the prime piece of we're after and the lumber to build the hotel."

Luke scrubbed his face with his hands, the bristly hair of his moustache a reminder he needed his friend's services. "Mind giving me a trim?" He pulled at the long hairs over the corners of his mouth.

Al stood. "Not at all." He set his cup of coffee on the crate. "Have a seat."

Lowering himself onto a straight-back chair sitting beside their small smoldering campfire, Luke watched as Al sharpened his razor on a large strap attached to whitewashed commode covered with nicks and gashes, markings of a life of travel.

"I said trim. Not shave it off."

"I thought I'd treat you to the works, might calm you down a bit." Al's hearty laugh brought a smile to Luke's face.

"Easy for you to say. Your woman didn't refuse..." Luke stopped midsentence. He couldn't finish—the thought left an irksome taste in his mouth. His not being a Christian wasn't a good reason to refuse his offer of courtship.

A cape snapped out and over him, then Al's fingers tucked it under his collar. Al stepped in front of him, working up a lather in his china shaving cup. The soft bristles of the brush applying the silky soap tickled his cheek.

"Tell me why you don't believe in God." Al applied the last dab of soap to Luke's skin.

Luke shook his head. "I just don't believe."

"Ah." Al set all his shaving supplies on the commode and crossed his arms. "I fell through ice when I was about ten. I was certain I was going to die so I started praying. Our farm dog saw me and kept nipping at my arm until he pulled me from the freezing water. The next Sunday I was saved."

"So you tricked me into a shave to preach to me?"

"No, to witness to you."

"Well, I prayed to God when I was little, too. He never answered any of my prayers. Now are you going to shave me or do I have to wipe the soap off on the cape?"

Al lifted the razor. "You have many of the qualities of a Christian. You know right from wrong. You're not afraid of hard work." He tipped his head.

Luke knew he was pondering how a heathen would demonstrate those traits. "Yeah, you might say those qualities were beaten into me."

Al raised his eyebrows.

The happy squeal of a baby cut through the area.

Luke could see Cora, Bertha and Henry approaching. Henry hung over Cora's arm, blue eyes peeked out of his bonnet. Henry smiled at Luke, making Luke's heart surge with happiness.

"I'm sorry. Are we interrupting?" Cora eyes glimmered in the July sun. "We know we're early for the celebration. We're so excited. We hurried through our chores."

The women each wore her hair braided and wrapped in knot at the base of her neck. A straw hat, decorated with pasque flowers and wild daisies, covered each of their heads, shielding their eyes from the blazing sun. Luke recognized their summer Sunday best—loose-fitting gauze dresses, Bertha's in blue and Cora's in lavender.

Bertha lifted the basket that normally held laundry. "I've got fried pheasant, boiled eggs, pickled beets, bread and tea." She looked around. "I was hoping someone would be selling ice."

"They are." Al relieved Bertha of the basket and tucked it into a tent out of the hot sun. "We can go get some when I've finished shaving Luke."

"Cora can shave Luke. She's very good. She had plenty of practice, first on her dad, then on Hank." Bertha rested her hand on Al's forearm and raised her brows. Luke couldn't be sure, but he thought he saw a sly smile flicker on both of their lips.

"I don't know." Cora jostled Henry from one arm to the other. "I'm sure Luke would prefer a professional shave."

"Not really." Luke's words popped out before he could stop them.

"I guess if you don't mind taking Henry, I can shave Luke." Cora pecked Henry's forehead and a deep blush prettied her cheeks.

"Splendid." Al took Henry from Cora and the trio started off.

Luke sensed Cora's reluctance to perform this intimate task. "You're dressed so pretty. Why don't I just shave myself?"

For a brief second their eyes met and he saw the spark of love glowing in her eyes before Cora lowered her gaze and turned to the commode, motioning for him to sit. "I won't make a mess."

He lowered his frame back to the chair. She picked up the straight razor and before Luke could protest again, she made a gentle glide up his cheek.

"Why, I hardly felt the razor's edge."

Cora smiled. "As Bertha told you, I've had a lot of practice."

Faint traces of lilac tickled his nose with Cora's precise movements. Luke leaned toward her, breathing deeply. Her soft hands stilled his movement. With short flicks of her wrist, the razor edged Luke's skin. Not one drip of soap fell on the cape or Cora.

Water swished when Cora ran the straightedge through it.

"You aren't even making a mess." His awe showed in his voice. "Even Al drips."

Cora giggled. "My father was bedridden the last few years of his life. If I dripped shaving cream or water on him or the bed linens, it meant changing them, which created more work for me. I was busy enough running the farm and the household. This will be easier if you'd stop talking and hold still.

The razor tickled his jawline, followed by tingling trails where Cora's fingers grazed his skin. She gently lifted his chin and ran the blade up his neck.

Through half-lidded eyes, Luke watched the concentration on Cora's face. He could get used to her soft hand cupping his cheek while the other removed a sign of his masculinity. The warm silkiness of her skin left him when she turned to wash the blade. He fancied Cora. Her nearness riled his insides. It took every ounce of his effort not to pull her onto his lap and kiss her.

He cleared his throat, hoping the action would also clear the thoughts in his head. "This is the first time you've spoken about your family. Where are they?"

"Buried in Ohio. Tilt." Cora tipped her own head in the direction she wanted his to go.

"I'm sorry."

"Thank you. It was a long time ago. My mother caught

a fever when I was young. My father had a stroke when I was fourteen. I managed to keep our farm going until he died two years later. After his death, the expenses mounted. The bank took the farm and I was left on my own without a home—until I married Hank."

"Is that the reason you want to prove up so badly?" Luke waited to ask the question until she turned to clean the razor.

"Yes. I'm not losing another home." Cora dipped a towel into a kettle of water Al had on the commode and began to wipe the residue from Luke's skin.

When she finished, she slipped her thumb and forefinger in the handle of a dainty pair of scissors and started snipping the hairs above his lip. Her green eyes, intent on their task, made his heart soar. He thought he'd offered to court her to protect her from Clement, but the honest truth was he wanted to court Cora. He wanted to make her his own. He wanted to be part of her family.

"Was your pa good to you?"

Surprise pulled Cora from her task. She knitted her brows. "Yes, he was." Then sadness veiled her eyes as she read his mind. "Didn't your father treat you well?"

"Well, well, well...have you taken up barbering, too?"

In an instant, Luke pulled Cora to his side. He stood, whipping the cape from his collar and letting it drop to the ground.

"What do you want?" Luke glowered at Clement.

Clement rubbed his face with his palm. "Thought maybe I needed a shave, too." His unnerving leer rested on Cora.

Luke's stomach flipped. He pushed Cora behind him and clenched his fists.

"Someone want a shave?" Al's voice cut through the tension. His eyes met Luke's then dropped to Luke's fists. He gave his head a slight shake.

Clement tipped his hat to Bertha. "You ladies look like a refreshing summer breeze in your finery."

Bertha scowled and walked over to Cora. "You've seen our Sunday dresses at church many times."

Her snappy answer brought a pucker of irritation to Clement's lips. Surprise flared in his eyes. He'd lost his ally and he knew it.

"I'm not after a shave. I actually stopped to tell you." Clement's eyes met Al's then Luke's. His lips curled into a sneer. "My lumber company won't be able to fill your order."

"What?" Luke's raised voice drew the attention of a passerby. He stepped toward Clement. Arms lifted. Hands fisted.

"You heard me. I can't fill the order."

Clement's nonchalant shrug ignited Luke's temper. Someone needed to teach this man a lesson. Luke pulled his arm back. Before he could step forward, a hand cupped his fist and pushed it down to his side.

Al stood beside him, shaking his head. "Do you mind telling us why you can't fill our order?"

"Your building, why, it's too big. If I give you all my lumber then the other good people won't be able to build. After all, I have to be fair."

"We placed our order before many of these people came." Luke spat out his words and waved an arm in the air. "We should get first consideration."

"Playing favorites wouldn't be very Christian of me, now would it?"

A growl hummed low in Luke's throat. If Clement was an example of a good Christian man, he was glad he wanted no part of God's family.

"I guess this town wasn't meant to be your home." Clement looped his thumbs through the suspenders under his jacket and puffed out his chest. He tipped his head to peer behind Luke and cast a menacing glance at Cora. "No sense bidding on land when there's not enough lumber to build."

"I'm going to bust your jaw." No one was telling him what to do anymore.

Luke's clenched-teeth threat removed the smile from Clement's face. He took a step back. Three cowhands standing in the crowd stepped forward until the four men formed a uniform line.

"Still want to fight?" Clement arched a snowy brow.

Al placed a steadying hand on Luke's shoulder. He lowered his arms and loosened his fists.

"You're doing this on purpose and I know why. You want to..."

"Ahem." Al cut Luke off midsentence. "Clement, is there anything we can do to change your mind?"

"No." Clement and his small band of men turned to go. Before he even took a step, he turned. "Maybe there is. If you—" he pointed to Luke "—can break a bronco in less time than I can in today's rodeo, the wood you ordered is yours. If not, I guess you'll be finding a new town to call home."

Luke sucked in a ragged breath. He had no idea how to ride a bucking horse. He'd do it, though—anything to see this dream through and protect Cora.

Al's hand squeezed his shoulder. "You don't have to do this, Luke. The Lord will provide."

Luke looked at Al. The earnestness on his face reflected his belief in his statement.

Luke snorted. "I don't believe I'll rely on the Lord." He turned to Clement. "You've got yourself a deal."

"Why'd you agree to compete against Clement?" Cora tugged on Luke's sleeve to get his attention. "He's the best bronco buster in this part of Dakota. You can't win."

Anger puckered her face and wrinkled her cute little nose.

"We need the lumber. He's trying to run us out of town so he can..." Luke stopped when horror replaced the anger on Cora's face.

"There are other ways to get lumber. Don't get on a bucking horse if you don't know what you're doing." Al's soft-spoken voice showed no hint of anger.

"Look, I've been run off my home by one man who hid behind God, and I'm not letting that happen again." Luke wagged his finger in Al's face.

"I can see where those circumstances would rile a man." Al nodded and didn't even seem to notice Luke's scolding finger. "There's no sense getting hurt over it."

"Al's right. Listen to him." Bertha face showed genuine concern. "Clement gets paid to bust broncos. He knows what he's doing."

Luke took a deep breath. He'd promised himself no one would treat him this way again. If he refused to ride in the rodeo, Clement would always have this weakness to hold over him. "I'm doing it, with or without your support."

He strode out into the crowded streets. *Family.* They always let you down when times got tough, he thought, as he headed in the direction of the rodeo grounds. He'd seen families so tight no one could break the bonds. If you fought with one you fought them all. He couldn't even get his family to back one decision, even if it was a bad one.

Luke stopped so suddenly he almost fell forward. The hot July sun must have baked his brain. The people he was angry with weren't his family. They were his friends. This lumber deal had his mind in a muddle. He took off his hat and wiped his palm across his forehead.

"Thank goodness." Cora planted herself in front of him. Puffing a little, she placed her hands on her hips. "It's not polite for a lady to run down Main Street."

The determined look on her face brought a smile to his lips. The deep crimson blush on her cheeks offset the facets of brown in her emerald eyes.

"You can't talk me out of this." He crooked his elbow and offered it to her. She slipped her gloved hand around his arm, the white lace a contrast on his blue shirt.

"Have you ever ridden a bucking horse?"

"No." Luke replied as they weaved around a group of people visiting at the side of the street.

"Well, then expect to get hurt."

Luke stopped and looked down at Cora. "I thought you were going to talk me out of it."

"No. You seem bent on doing this, so I'll be here to cheer you on and tend your wounds."

A swirling joy spun around Luke's heart, expanding until he thought his chest might burst. "Really?"

Cora's smiled widened. She nodded her head. "That is what friends do."

*Friends.* The word sucked at his mind. He loved Cora and wanted to be part of her family, not just her friend. Yet, she'd been firm. He had to believe in God if he wanted courting privileges. Luke swallowed hard. It was something he couldn't do. He resumed walking toward the rodeo arena.

"I wish I had some knowledge of breaking horses to give you."

"Don't worry about it. The advice probably wouldn't help much, anyway. I think it's something you learn with experience." Luke placed his free hand over Cora's lacey one. "It's nice knowing you're on my side."

"It's the least I can do after all you've done for us."

The clamor of a horse's hooves drew Luke's attention away from Cora's pretty eyes. He stopped and stepped in front of Cora seconds before a rider raced past the throng of people in the street. Luke frowned. He recognized the rider. It was one of Clement's hired men and he had an odd contraption attached to his saddle.

"I wonder where he's going in such a hurry." Cora brushed dust from the skirt of her dress.

"Isn't he one of Clement's men?" Luke watched the rider distance himself from the town, growing smaller until he was a dot on the horizon.

"Yes, he's one of Clement's men. Why?"

"Did you notice his saddle?"

Lilting giggles bubbled from Cora. "Yes, he's afraid of the dark. Keeps a lantern lit when he's riding at night. The extra piece of leather is so it doesn't burn his horse if he needs both hands on the reins. It's quite something to see at night."

*I believe I have.* Luke thought of his early-morning ride to Cora's homestead. Not wanting to give Cora cause to worry, Luke chuckled. "I bet it is. Funny he hasn't set himself or the countryside on fire." Luke smiled down at Cora, whose face was alive with merriment. "Let's go get me signed up to ride and take a look at the horses."

"You do know you don't have to go through with this. Al won't mind."

"Cora, I need to do this."

She nodded her head and walked along in silence.

Scanning the horizon, Luke decided there was something else he needed to do—take a ride around the outskirts of Clement's property to see if any sheep were grazing with Clement's cattle.

# Chapter 11

The din of the crowd made it hard to hear. Cora turned and scanned the group of spectators, certain someone had called her name.

"Cora."

She saw Al waving his hat.

"Pardon me." Cora sucked in her breath and squeezed past the people lining the fence separating the rodeo arena from the crowd. Turning and sidestepping, Cora worked her way over to Al and Bertha.

"Where's Luke?" Urgency sounded in Al's voice.

"In there, waiting to ride." Cora pointed to the dirt arena. "Why?"

"He doesn't have to compete." Al stretched to his full height. "I don't see him."

On tiptoes, Cora tried to locate Luke among the group of men who'd signed up to break broncos. She was too short to see over the people who stood in front of her.

"I found lumber. He doesn't have to go through with this foolish bet."

"You found lumber!" Cora clapped her hands together. "Where?"

"Reverend Beacom knows the man who runs the yard in Dunnebeck. The lumberman is here celebrating the Fourth of July. He expects another load of lumber next week and is willing to sell it to us at a better price than Clement. There's one hitch. We need to pick it up." Al gently traded places with Cora during his explanation.

Cora unburdened Bertha of Henry. His body heat radiated into her gauze dress.

"Why don't you ladies find some shade to stand in to watch the rodeo? I'm going to try to get inside, find Luke and stop this foolishness."

Bertha led Cora out of the crowd. Together they walked toward a grove of trees by the end of the fencing.

"I don't see Al." Bertha squinted and leaned into the fence. "I hope he doesn't get hurt trying to stop your man."

"Bertha!" Cora was astonished that Bertha referred to Luke as her suitor.

A sheepish grin tugged at Bertha's lips. "Al and I know he wants to court you."

Henry gurgled.

"See? Henry agrees."

"Enough." Cora sounded like a schoolmarm warning her class. "You know Luke isn't a Christian."

Sobering, Bertha nodded. "I know. Shall we pray neither of our friends gets hurt?"

"Oh, yes." Cora grabbed Bertha's hand. "Heavenly Father, protect Al and Luke from harm. Help Al to locate Luke. Give him the right words to talk Luke out of this foolishness. Help Luke come to know You as the loving Father that You are. Amen."

Cora opened her eyes. The action had started. A chestnut quarter horse kicked its hind legs over and over. A skinny cowboy bounced around in the saddle and remained upright. The crowd roared and clapped.

"It doesn't really look hard." Cora tilted her head. "Maybe Luke will be okay after all."

As the words left her mouth, the horse twisted to the right and the cowboy flew sideways, landing on his head and shoulders in the hard dirt.

"Still think so?"

Cora shook her head at Bertha.

It took several minutes to get the horse ready for the next rider. Cora sent up silent prayers for Luke's safety. Although Luke had a temper and worked hard, he didn't have the same rough edge these pioneer men shared. It was one of the things she loved about him.

She grimaced at her thoughts. She tried hard, but couldn't control her feelings for Luke. They were too strong.

When cheers filled the air, Cora opened her eyes. The cowboys surrounding the horse parted. One man held the horse steady while the rider secured his stance in the saddle.

"It's Luke." Cora's knees weakened. She grabbed hold of the fence for support with her free hand. The man holding the bridle let go. Time stilled. The bronco's first back-legged buck sent Luke's citified hat whirling through the air. For seconds it seemed suspended, like the sun in the sky, before it fell.

The horse reared up. Its front hooves clawed the air. Luke slid back. He kept his place on the saddle until the horse's forelegs hit the ground, then he bounced forward. His hair flopped over his face, his curls covering his eyes.

Wooziness washed over Cora. Thinking she might faint, she tried to inhale deeply when she realized she'd been holding her breath. Exhaling, she drew several deep breaths.

The horse began to run. Luke stuck with him. Occasionally, it kicked its back legs, but not with the same height or force it previously had.

"I believe he's breaking it." Cora looked to Bertha.

"It appears so."

The horse began to trot. Luke rode the horse around the arena until its stride turned to a slower lope. The crowd whooped and whistled. Luke let go of the reins with one hand and waved.

Cora and Bertha joined the happy chorus of cheers and hollers. Spectators threw their hats in the arena. One landed in front of the bronco. The horse shied and abruptly changed course, knocking Luke off balance. In an instant, he slid off the side of the horse.

A whoop caught in Cora's throat. She grabbed the fence, watching for a sign of movement. Surely falling with such ease wouldn't harm him. She waited. No movement. Her pulse pounded in her ears.

Her heart urged her to climb the fence and run to him. She lifted a foot to the bottom cross board and hefted herself and Henry a few inches higher. A crowd of men had gathered around Luke, making it impossible for her to see.

Henry bounced against her chest with each heaving breath she took. Tears sprang to her eyes. Was he hurt badly? Her heart dropped and her stomach lurched. She stretched her torso over the fence.

"Come down from there. You'll hurt my grandson and yourself." Bertha put her hands around Cora's waist to keep her steady. Cora stepped down.

Concern etched Bertha's features. "We need to get to the rider's entrance if we want to know what's going on."

Bertha had a firm grip on Cora's elbow, leading her back into the crowd of onlookers.

Everything happened so fast—Cora's thoughts twisted and spun like the bucking horse trying to free itself of the saddle and rider. Her heart's frantic beating only added to her frenzied thoughts. She needed to get to Luke. She needed to help him. She needed to tell him she loved him.

*Loved him.* Her knees weakened. She stumbled under Bertha's firm grip. "Stop."

Bertha did and turned. "Are you all right? You're so pale."

"Take Henry." Cora held her gurgling son out. Once he was safe in Bertha's arms, Cora doubled over trying to catch her breath and stop her racing heart. She shouldn't love Luke. He wasn't a Christian.

The railroad officials stood on the raised floor of the depot. Several workers looked through the framework of the building to ensure they didn't miss a bid. They'd marked and numbered the lots and planned to auction the land in numerical order.

Luke's wrist throbbed. Sheer will had kept him glued to the bucking horse's saddle. The same will had helped him endure his father's punishments for falling short. The same will helped him work since he was twelve to save money for his dream. The same will was helping him stand upright for the land auction.

Sweat beaded around Luke's hatband and trickled down the sides of his face. The sling his arm rested in blanketed his body in the sweltering summer heat, adding to his misery. The lots he and Al planned to purchase were four and five, so he shouldn't have to stand much longer in the blazing sun.

"Are you okay?"

Looking down into Cora's green eyes filled with concern, Luke's heart jumped in his chest. Since he'd broken his wrist, Cora seemed to view him in a different light. Her normally shining eyes were clouded with an emotion he couldn't pinpoint. Disappointment? How could she be disappointed in him? He'd stayed on the horse long enough to break it, forcing Clement to keep his word on delivering the lumber. Shouldn't pride shine in her eyes when she looked at him?

"I'm fine." He nodded his head. The medicine the doctor gave him for the pain only took the edge off.

She pursed her lips. "You don't look fine." She handed him a handkerchief. "Wipe your brow."

Little Henry groaned and strained in her arms, reaching his hands for Luke. It broke his heart he couldn't scoop the little man into his arms. It was all he could do to hold up his own weight. He'd never want to drop or hurt Henry.

"Want me to do the bidding?" Al turned to Luke.

Luke nodded.

Once the railroad officials started the auction, the bidding moved fast. Most of the prospective landowners had a gentleman's agreement not to bid against each other. There was plenty of land for everyone who wanted a new start.

Luke looked down at Cora and Henry. A protective and soft feeling flooded through him. When he'd followed the railroad and heard about the terminus, he knew it was his chance to have a business of his own, to make something of his life. He hadn't counted on falling in love with a woman let alone a baby boy.

Love? Dizziness swirled through Luke. His frame made a small circle before he brought it into balance. He looked up at the sun's glare, then wiped his face again with Cora's hanky, the sweet smell of lilac water releasing from the warmth of his face.

Light-headed, Luke steeled his body. He had to fight his feelings. He'd vowed never to be part of a family again. And Cora had made it plain—she'd only love a believer, which was something he'd never become.

The whoops of the small group surrounding him brought him back to the present. Al patted his back and Cora squeezed his forearm.

"The land we wanted is ours. Our new life has started." Happiness creased every line in Al's face.

"Congratulations, Luke. You can start building your hotel."

Luke waited for the happy news to sink in, a feeling of accomplishment to wash through him, bringing peace to his soul. The feeling never came. Happiness always seemed to elude him.

He managed a weak smile.

"I think we need to get Luke out of the hot sun." Cora turned and led the way out of the crowd of people around the depot.

Back at their tent site, sitting under the shade of a maple tree, Cora lifted a quart canning jar filled with clear well water, poured some into a coffee cup and handed it to Luke. He sagged onto a crate and drank every drop.

"I'll talk to Clement about delivering the lumber today." Luke looked to Al.

"I'll take care of it. You need to rest so your broken wrist can heal." Al took the slice of bread and jam Bertha offered him and passed it to Luke.

"Speaking of which, I've hired someone to help me start building right away."

Luke's head snapped up. He chewed a bite of the airy bread and tart wild plum jam. "We don't have the money to hire anyone. In few days, I'll be able to help you."

Al shook his head. "No, you won't. This won't cost us any money. I've done a little bartering."

"He's very skilled at bartering." Cora chuckled. "Our pantry is filled with canned pheasant and rabbit."

Bertha beamed with pride at Al. "And he has the whitest barbering towels and capes in the county."

"Yes, I do." Al chuckled, too, and turned to Luke. "The young preacher is an experienced builder. He's going to help us build in trade for using the dining room for Sunday services until he can raise money to erect a church."

"What?" Luke stood so fast the crate toppled over. He fisted the hand in the sling. Pain shot through his left wrist and knocked the wind from his lungs. Wincing, he doubled over.

Al rushed to his side. He righted the crate and guided Luke into a sitting position. "Put those fists of yours away."

"I'm not having church in my establishment."

"We're partners, Luke. We need the help and having Sunday services in the dining room won't hurt anyone, including you. Besides, the townspeople will look right favorable on us if we allow them a roof over their heads for worship."

"No." Luke looked up. The shocked horror on Cora's face turned to disappointment. Her lips pursed and deep sadness settled in her green eyes. Luke's heart lurched. He looked from face to face. He could see how important this was to all of them, yet there was no room for God in his life or his establishment.

He knew the beliefs held by Cora, Bertha and Al were different than those he'd been raised with. To them, God meant love not punishment. Maybe the new preacher's beliefs were the same. The fact remained most of the churchgoing folks he knew acted like his father and Clement. They touted the virtues of God, yet their private actions held little humanity. He'd grown tired of the hypocrites.

Anger and a few moments of rest strengthened Luke's resolve. He stood and stepped in front of Al. Eyes narrowed and jaw set, he spoke through clenched teeth. "I won't have it." Then he waited, braced for the rod that mustn't be spared to the disobedient child.

Al's nostrils flared. His deep breath, ragged, cut through the silence. "I didn't say you had to attend. The young preacher knows you're resistant. We're willing to compromise, work things out."

There was firmness in Al's voice, but no hint of menace. His stature didn't change.

Luke backed up a step.

"Perhaps we should go back to the homestead." Cora, eyes round with disbelief, turned to Bertha.

"Please don't leave, ladies. You brought a nice picnic lunch for us to celebrate our purchase. I truly believe we have reason to celebrate. Don't you, Luke?" Al gave him a pointed look.

A pang of shame shot through Luke. His anger had almost spoiled a wonderful reason to celebrate. He and Al were landowners, businessmen and partners. They were bound to disagree at times, weren't they? He'd seen Cora and Bertha disagree, yet their relationship remained close.

"Yes, yes, of course it's cause to celebrate." Luke took a few steps back. Al maintained the same stance as before Luke's temper got the best of him. "I beg your pardon, ladies."

Both women gave their heads a small nod. Luke sat down on the crate, wondering if Al planned to thrash him after the women returned to their homestead. "I think I can hold Henry if you'd like me to."

"I think he wants you to." Cora placed the boy in the crook of Luke's arm. "He's been reaching for you all day."

Al arranged a blanket on the ground close to Luke. Cora and Bertha placed a basket in the middle of the blanket and spread a small feast out before them.

"How are you going to eat while holding Henry?" Bertha reached for the baby. Henry's lips turned into a pout. He started to whimper.

"You go ahead and eat. I had the bread and jam." Luke bounced his knee. Henry settled down and cuddled into him. Luke's heart sighed at the wonderful warmth the boy's gesture created inside and out.

"Ladies, you have outdone yourselves. This is the best kuchen I've ever tasted."

Bertha beamed. "It's an old family recipe."

Cora smiled and tilted her head. "I know this is none of my business. If you don't want to be around while the preacher is here helping Al, you could come out to the homestead. Once your wrist heals a little, you could probably hoe one-handed."

"Or even pick some of the vegetables. The green beans and peas will be mature and ready in a week or so," Bertha added.

"Those are splendid ideas, ladies. There are many solutions to our problem. All it takes is a little compromise." Al popped a hard-boiled egg into his mouth.

Luke shook his head at all the suggested solutions to the building situation. He looked down at Henry, who dozed peacefully in his arms. Protectiveness bubbled in him. He couldn't ever imagine striking his child.

*His child.* Luke's heart ached worse than his tightly bound broken wrist. He loved Henry, considered the boy his own, but that would never be true. He couldn't share

Cora's Christian beliefs and now that the town was growing, Cora would surely find someone to court her.

"What do you think, Luke?"

"What?" Luke tore his gaze from Henry.

"Would you mind going out to the homestead to help the ladies with chores while the young preacher helps me build our establishment?"

"No, I don't mind. After I heal some, I'd be more help here. I can hold boards or carry them to you." Luke shrugged. "I'll help out wherever I'm needed and on Sundays I guess I can head out to the homestead and do the morning chores."

Surprise registered on all the faces looking back at him.

"Well, then, it's settled." Cora stood and took Henry from his arms.

"Yes, it is. Not another word about it, right?" Al looked at Luke.

He nodded his head. He'd never experienced a confrontation or difference of opinion that wasn't settled physically. He looked at his arm in the sling. Had he listened to Al a week ago, he'd have the use of both his arms.

After laying Henry on the blanket, Cora lifted a plate. "Tell me what you'd like to eat."

"A couple of hard-boiled eggs, more bread and jam and a slice of the kuchen."

Cora pulled a crate beside him. "I'll hold the plate while you eat. When you want a sip of water, let me know."

"I think I can do this myself."

"Luke, you've helped me out so many times. Let me do this for you." The July sun couldn't outshine Cora's bright smile.

He nodded and removed an egg from the plate.

People began milling through town. Happy cheers and whoops filled the air.

Reverend Beacom stood on the fringes of their campsite. "Congratulations on getting your property."

"Thank you." Al stood and walked over to him with an outstretched hand. "Come in and share some lunch with us."

"I can't stay. I stopped by to wish you well and to ask those in my congregation to pray for the Grays. They've lost their homestead."

Luke stopped eating when he noted the concern on Cora's pretty face.

"What's happened?"

"Apparently, a couple of fighting bucks got into their corn and tore it up. They needed the crop to prove up."

Al and Luke exchanged a knowing look.

"What are they going to do?" Worry intoned Cora's question.

Luke knew she had faith in proving up her homestead, yet with every ounce of his being, he believed Clement was going to try to stop her. Luke braced for the answer he knew would come.

"Clement's offered to buy them out."

## Chapter 12

Fear lumped in Cora's throat. She swallowed hard. Her efforts moved her fright to the center of her chest, where it swiftly grew into a large, fierce swarm of worry. What would she feed her livestock if deer tore up her field of sorghum? Would the government consider her improvements enough to grant her ownership of the land? Of course not. One of the rules was homesteaders had to bring in a crop. She chewed her lower lip.

"They're sure mule deer tore up the crops?"

She stopped biting her lip when she heard the skepticism in Al's voice.

Before Reverend Beacom had a chance to respond, Clement rode up and stopped in front of their small group. Remaining mounted, he looked down at them. His eyes roamed Luke from head to toe before resting on the sling. Amusement gleamed in his eyes. His superiority tugged at his lips until they curled into a smug smile.

"Reverend." Clement tipped his hat. "Have you considered my offer to hold church services in the warehouse of the lumberyard? I'd be honored to have the word of the Lord delivered in my establishment."

The flinch of Luke's shoulders caught Cora's eyes. She stood at the wrong angle to tell if he was in pain or was reacting to Clement's offer. She slowly stepped closer to him, trying not to draw Clement's attention.

"No, thank you. Luke and Al promised to let me hold Sunday worship service in their dining room in exchange for my help building their establishment. Plus, they've offered me lodging."

"What?" Luke's astonishment was clear in his voice and the abrupt way he turned to Al.

"I gave him my area. I can bunk in the barbershop."

A disgusted snort cut through the tension. Cora waited for Luke's hands to fist, but they didn't.

"My warehouse has plenty of room." Clement leaned over the saddle horn, a smile fixed to his lips, but anger clouding his eyes.

"I'm sure it does. However, I gave my word to these gentlemen."

Clement opened his mouth to reply. Luke cut him off. "Where's our lumber? I broke the horse."

"So you did." Clement pulled at the edge of his moustache and grinned. "And your wrist, too."

Cora's gaze immediately dropped to Luke's hand. His fingers started to curl at Clement's goading.

"I don't see anything funny about an injury." Her thoughts flew from her mouth before she could stop them.

Clement cocked an eyebrow at her. "I beg your pardon, Cora. I didn't mean to imply Luke's broken bone was comical. You have to admit your friend here is not a rough-and-tumble man. He'd never be able to run a homestead, make it prosper or increase the land, which is what it seems you are trying to do."

"I *am* proving up my homestead." Cora felt her own hands clench. She placed her fists on her hips in what she hoped was a show of authority.

"Well, I guess so." Clement shrugged. "I'd hate to see you in the same predicament your neighbors ended up in, so close to proving up. Have you heard..."

"Yes." The word hissed off Cora's lips. "We have."

"No need to get snippy when a man's trying to ask permission to court you. Together, we can prove up your homestead. Keep a roof over the babe's head." Clement nodded toward the blanket.

Motherly instinct exploded in Cora. "I'm doing a fine job of maintaining our home and the agreement with the land office. All of my son's needs are met. I've told you before, Mr. Dykstra, I am in mourning."

Cora raised her voice so all those around them heard her refuse Clement's courting offer.

The narrow-eyed stare Clement pinned on her sent chills crawling up her back. He jutted out his chin. He opened his mouth and, looking around, his eyes rested on the reverend. He pursed his lips. Sitting back in the saddle, he tipped his hat. "I beg your pardon, Cora. I'll call on you again in October. I believe September marks a year."

He spurred his horse and called over his shoulder, "I'll send my boys over with the lumber. Reverend, if you change your mind about the warehouse, let me know."

Intense quivers worked their way up her calves, knocking her knees together. Clement was never going to leave her alone, even if she proved up the homestead. Her problems wouldn't end with the deed to her property. She'd always have to deal with Clement.

Her shaking legs weakened. "I think I need to sit down."

All three men moved toward her, but it was Luke's strong arm that caught her the moment her legs buckled.

Luke led her to the blanket and helped ease her down onto the scratchy wool.

"I've been a fool. I should have told Clement from the very beginning I'd never allow him to court me, mourning or not."

Luke squatted beside her, his broken wrist resting on his knee. She looked into his brown eyes. "Even if I prove up the homestead, Bertha, Henry and I won't be safe." She shivered. The July sun blazed hot, however the stark reality in her words chilled her to the bone.

"I won't let him harm you."

Luke's words, low and firm, were meant to reassure her. Instead, another round of icy tremors overtook her body.

"Allow me to court you. He'll get the message and leave you alone." Wrapping his arm around her shoulder, he held her trembling body tight to his side.

Cora's heart jumped with longing. She'd imagined him asking her this question again after he'd accepted Christ as his Savior. The dream filled her waking and sleeping hours. She wanted to say yes. Fling her arms around him and let love's bubbly happiness overtake her, but she couldn't. The Lord blessed her with such abundance. She must remain faithful to Him and His word.

Besides, Henry needed a good Christian example to follow. Bitter tears burned her eyes. "I can't. We can't. You're not..."

Stammering, she pulled away from his embrace, watching the hope evaporate from his face like water drops on a cookstove top. He lowered his eyes, and gave his head a shake. Cora knew she didn't need to finish her sentence.

Luke dumped the dregs of his coffee onto the morning campfire, the bitterness no match for the taste Cora's refusal left in his mouth. It'd been three days and the situation weighed heavier than ever on his mind.

He knew her feelings matched his in strength and depth. He saw the warring in her eyes. Her reason for denying his offer was a foolish one. He'd treat her right, keep her family safe. What difference did it make if he believed in God? His father and Clement were both believers and poor examples of men.

Luke sighed and ran his fingers through his hair. He watched Al and Reverend Beacom sort boards. They were Christians. Their kindness showed in their words and actions, actions completely the opposite of his father's and Clement's. Maybe not all Christians were hypocrites. Perhaps he'd been wrong about God as well.

He rubbed the stiff stubble on his chin. One-handed shaving was difficult, yet he couldn't ask Al for a shave. He fancied Cora's abilities with a razor over Al's anyway, the softness of her palm cupping his cheek, the faint smell of lilac on her skin.

Luke sighed. He had to stop thinking and acting foolish. He'd allowed Clement to goad him into riding the bucking horse, now Al bore the burden of building the hotel. Yet, not once had he complained or blamed Luke for his circumstances. Al was a fine man.

Placing his hat on his head, Luke walked over to the two men. "How's it going?"

"He gave us crooked boards." Al's disgust showed in his voice. "We can't use bent boards for the foundation or the framing."

"It won't hurt to use them on the façade." Reverend Beacom wiped his brow with a hanky. "And we might be able to pound some straight for the sides."

"I don't know." Al shrugged. "What do you want to do?"

Luke shook his head. Their funds were tight. All the

money he had left he planned to use on the hotel furnishings. "Think you can still get lumber from your contact in Dunnebeck?"

"Probably." Al frowned. "How are we going to pay for it?"

"I guess with the money I set aside for furnishings." Luke sighed.

"Gentleman, I suggest we pray about this."

Luke's stance stiffened.

Reverend Beacom held up his hands. "In our own ways. I'm not pushing God on you, Luke. I'm saying He does provide for his children. Al is a good hunter. I understand you have a thriving garden at the homestead. Congregants bring me what they can for my sustenance, which I'm willing to share. Al has a steady income with his barbering."

Al brightened. "You're right. We don't have to worry about buying food. My business will pick up when more people move to town, not to mention those passing through. We'll be able to buy those furnishings."

"Praise God from whom all blessings flow." The reverend nodded his head at Al. "Amen." Al smiled.

They talked so easily about God. Cora and Bertha did, too. They didn't shout scripture, preach punishment and pound their fists. Luke shook his head in disbelief.

"I'll try to get word to the lumberman in Dunnebeck this afternoon. We can start building the façade today."

"Okay, I think I'll ride out to the homestead." Luke adjusted the sling around his neck.

"Have you seen anything suspicious?"

Al and Luke exchanged looks at the Reverend Beacom's question.

"I've heard the rumblings of gossip. Those homesteaders think Clement's behind their troubles. I saw the look you two shared. You think so, too."

"Cora's had trouble with him. He's tried to force her into marriage since her husband died." Al shook his head. "I think he's up to no good."

"It's the reason I didn't want to hold services on his property. I've seen his kind before in the West."

Luke snorted. "How? You're barely older than me."

"My father's a Texas Ranger and my brother's a marshal in this area. I've seen all kinds of folks, heard all kinds of stories."

"Why didn't you go into law enforcement?"

Reverend Beacom shrugged. "I thought I could do more good saving souls. I've been thinking about wiring my brother about the situation here. See if some temporary law enforcement can come to Faith, at least until the town gets established and hires a sheriff."

"Good idea." Luke tipped his head in respect to the reverend. "I haven't seen anything funny going on at Cora's since the spring. I rode around the circumference of Clement's ranch. I didn't see any sheep."

"Doesn't mean he didn't take them or butcher them." Al crossed his arms over his chest.

"I know. Since the ladies rounded them up and penned them closer to the house they haven't lost one."

Luke adjusted his suspender under his sling. "I'll be anxious to know what you find out about the lumber."

He walked to his horse. Grabbed the reins, pushed his boot in the stirrup, swung his body up and winced in pain until he sat upright in the saddle.

He kept his horse at an easy lope, riding down the line staked out for the railroad tracks, which ran adjacent to Cora and her former neighbor's property. He'd ridden this route for the last three days not seeing one mule deer, confirming his suspicion about the torn-up field. Today, he'd try to set Cora's mind at ease about her crop.

Turning his horse, he rode across the homestead Clement had recently purchased, looking for signs of anything suspicious. When he didn't find anything, he rode along the rocky crags bordering Clement's and Cora's property.

His horse whinnied, stopped and started to back up. The faint breeze wafted a bitter scent through the air. Blood. Luke regained control of his horse, guiding him toward the edge of the rocky crags. He proceeded with caution. Rounding a small rock formation, Luke squinted. The sun glimmered off something shiny.

Luke backed the horse into a cavern in the rock created by an overhang. A few feet away another horse grazed on vegetation growing from between the rocks. As that horse turned its body to get a better grip on the prairie grass, Luke saw what had reflected the sunbeams. A lantern.

The horse belonged to Clement's hand. Another breeze brought a sickening smell. Luke swallowed hard and pulled his handkerchief from his pocket to cover his nose and mouth. The acrid scent of blood filled the air.

Luke tapped his heels to move his horse out of the shadow of the crags. The hand's horse moved, giving Luke a full view of its rider. Clement's hired hand deftly worked a knife up and down. He was butchering something. One of Cora's sheep?

Unable to inch closer without being seen, Luke backed his mount up several steps before turning it around. Making slow progress, Luke chose a route that wrapped around another formation.

His wrist throbbed with each jarring step on the uphill climb. Finally, the horse reached a small plateau, giving Luke the advantage of looking down on the hand. His eyes narrowed, his jaw set. The man wasn't slaughtering one of Cora's sheep. He was butchering two mule deer.

This confirmed it. Clement was behind the demise of

Cora's neighbor's homesteads. How they'd captured and got the mule deer into the field was beyond Luke. Butchering the bucks out here, where coyotes would get rid of the carcasses, eliminated any evidence of foul play. Or were they doing this on Cora's land to make it appear as if she'd had a part in this scheme? Had they captured, killed and left Cora's missing sheep for the coyotes' dinner this spring, attempting to thin her herd and making it impossible for her to prove up her homestead?

Carefully, Luke descended the rocks. He guided his horse across the prairie leading to the back side of Cora's land. He'd need Al to come out and scout around for better tracks and signs of foul play on Cora's property.

Worry for Cora, Bertha and Henry's safety gnawed at his gut. He steeled his resolve the closer he rode to the farmhouse so Cora wouldn't see his concern.

Due to his broken wrist, he could spend days at the homestead. Keep his eye on things.

It was the nights that troubled his mind. Did Clement and his hands slink around in the darkness, carrying out their plans to ruin the homesteaders? So far, he hadn't physically harmed anyone, just stolen their hopes and dreams of a home by taking their land.

Disgust replaced worry at the lengths a man would go to for riches. Soon Clement would own many acres of land and a thriving business, sacrificing relationships with neighbors, friends and family.

Luke's eyes widened. He wanted to build a business and make money. Did that make him and Clement the same type of person?

His heart pounded against his ribs. He didn't want to own everything, only one business—the hotel—a business to give him security and fill his lonely hours.

Luke sighed. A family filled a man's lonely hours. He'd

never thought so before. Now he knew it was true. Cora and
Henry had changed his mind. Bertha and Al, too. He cared
about them in the way he suspected blood family feels. He
missed them when he wasn't with them. He enjoyed their
company. He loved them. And he'd do whatever he needed
to protect them and their home.

His eyes went heavenward. God was real. Was this the
answer to his long-ago prayers to stop the pain and let love
enter his heart?

With little guidance from him, his horse walked to the
main path that led to Cora's house, seeming to know his
way home. Stunned at his thoughts, Luke shook his head
in an attempt to clear it.

Both women, faces reddened from the washtub's steam,
carried heaped clothes baskets from the sod house when
Luke rode up to the barn. He slipped from his horse and
tethered it to a hitching post.

"Good morning."

The sun glistened on Cora's chestnut hair, deep shades of
auburn shimmered like rubies in its brightness. The breeze
danced a loose ringlet across her forehead and into her eyes.
She set the basket on the ground and pulled her fingers
through the loose hair, tucking it behind her ear.

Luke's fingers itched to anchor the ringlet, trace the out-
line of her dainty ear.

"Ladies." He tipped his hat. "Al sends his best."

A wide smile crinkled Bertha's face. "I'll take care of
these clothes. The sun has moved and Henry's no longer
in the shade. Take him in and start lunch."

Cora retrieved Henry from a basket beside the sod house
and walked to the pump.

Henry smiled and cooed, waving his hand at the fingers
Luke waggled at him.

Luke followed Cora to the pump. She hooked a bucket

on the spigot. Luke pumped the handle a few times before a gush of clear, cool water splashed out.

Cora started to lift the bucket.

"I'll get it." Wincing a little, Luke carried the filled bucket into the house, glad he followed Cora and she couldn't see his weakness.

He'd grown accustomed to making himself at home. Luke placed the bucket on a shelf in the pantry, removed an enamel cup from its station and skimmed it across the water. Drawing back the burlap curtain, he stepped from the pantry while he took a sip of the cool liquid, the best in the territory. He offered the cup to Cora.

"Thank you." She took the cup and drank the remaining water. "I expected you earlier."

Luke sat at the table and motioned for Cora to hand him Henry. She placed him on Luke's knee. Henry's bright blue eyes looked up at Luke with such trust; emotion welled in his own eyes. How could anyone hurt a child the way his father had? He wrapped his arm around Henry, pulling him into a tight hug and making a silent promise no one would hurt Henry. The child rested his head on Luke's chest. A contented feeling washed through him.

"Oh!"

The sound a breathy sigh more than a word, Luke looked up to find Cora staring at them, fingers over her mouth. Her face wore the same expression as the night Henry was born. Her gaze met his. He recognized the emotion—love.

A small smile played on her lips. Another wave of emotion grew in his chest, pushing happiness to every limb in his body. Only one thing could make this moment better. The feel of Cora's arms wrapped around his waist, her head resting on his shoulder.

Luke stood, secured Henry in the crook of his arm and took a step toward Cora. A veil of sadness settled on her face. She blinked her eyes several times before turning away from him.

"Cora." The tremble in his voice sounded strange. He cleared his throat and moved across the floor. He wanted to touch her shoulder, turn her toward him. With Henry in one arm and the other in a sling, he was unable to. "Cora, please look at me."

She turned. Whatever warred inside her showed on her face, erasing her earlier love-filled expression. He longed to see the love again, needed to see it again. He motioned for her to take Henry. When she lifted the child from his uninjured arm, he wrapped it around her, drawing her close.

The warmth of her body soaked into him, giving him a strength he'd never felt before. He needed this and after what he'd seen today, she needed his protection. He loosened his hold. She tipped her face up. Her lips parted.

He knew what she planned to say and he didn't want to hear it. There was better use for her lips. He dipped his head and kissed her.

## Chapter 13

Cora yielded to Luke's soft lips. The wonderful rush of love swirled through her, filling every inch of her heart until it pattered a happy tune in her chest. She leaned into him, encouraging him to continue kissing her, even though she shouldn't. His kiss deepened.

Everything in Cora's mind narrowed, focusing on his soft lips and the surge of love coursing through every ounce of her soul. Her spirit sang loud and strong, rivaling many a church choir's halleluiahs.

*Church.*

*God.*

The words triggered her mind, expanded her thoughts and squelched love's thrill. Her racing heart sputtered, changing its skittering pace to a dull thud. Luke never spoke his love for her, but his kiss proved he fancied her, returned her feelings of love. Yet, they had no chance at a future together. He didn't share her Christian beliefs. She must stop giving in to her feelings. Her love for Luke was her weakness. She placed her hands on Luke's chest and pushed away. Confusion replaced the flush of love on his handsome face.

"Luke, I can't." A curl loosened when she shook her head, tumbling across her eyes. "We can't." She lifted her hand to tuck the hair back into place. Luke beat her to it.

His fingertips brushed her forehead, sending tickling tingles down her cheek.

"I've wanted to run my fingers through your hair since the night Henry was born."

The huskiness of his voice sent shivers galloping through her body.

The corners of Luke's mouth turned down, giving him a forlorn look. He stuck the curl behind her ear. "You don't have to say it. I know the verse. You can't be yoked with an unbeliever. It's 2nd Corinthians, Chapter 6, Verse 14."

Only when Luke moved his fingers under her chin and pushed up did Cora realize her mouth gaped open in astonishment. Luke knew the Bible!

She wrinkled her brow and palmed her forehead. Had the world blurred? "How do you know Scripture, if you aren't a believer?" she whispered.

"Memorization saved me from the strap more than once."

"I don't understand."

"It doesn't really matter." Luke pulled his gaze from her face and stared into the distance. "You believe what the Bible says is true." Sadness intoned Luke's words.

Happy laughter sounded outside the door. Luke scooped Henry from her arms. His boots scuffed across the wood floor. He walked to the window.

"Al's here." Concern filled his voice.

Bertha led the way into the house. "I thought lunch would be ready. Oh, well. We'll get it together in no time."

She stepped toward Cora, who hadn't fully come out of her daze. Luke once believed in God?

"Cora, you slice the bread and I'll slice the leftover pheasant from Sunday's dinner." Bertha bustled around the pantry, handing items to Cora.

She took the bread and a knife to the table and began to slice through the dense loaf.

"Cora, are you okay?"

"Yes. Why?" She met Al's eyes. Surely he couldn't tell she and Luke had shared a kiss.

"Those are pretty thick slices of bread." He reached for the knife.

Sighing, Cora looked down at the loaf, then released the handle of the knife into Al's hand.

"I came out to tell Luke we are able to get better lumber, however, we need to start out this afternoon."

"What?" Luke had been staring into space.

"I got word today our lumber is ready in Dunnebeck. I thought if Cora and Bertha didn't mind, we'd borrow their buckboard. You and Reverend Beacom can go get it. I'll stay here, do some barbering in town during the day, and come out to help the ladies garden in the evening."

"Oh, what wonderful news. Of course you can take the wagon. We won't have this batch of laundry ready to deliver for two days. Do you need to use Dutch?" Cora smoothed imaginary wrinkles from her apron.

"If you don't mind, we would."

"Why don't you and the preacher go? I'll stay and help with the gardening. I can't load the lumber anyway." Luke winced when he lifted his hurt arm, making Cora want to rush to his side, adjust the sling, help to ease his pain.

She lowered her eyes to the floor and gave her head

a small shake, trying to stop her heart from ruling her thoughts.

"That's why you're going. You can drive the wagon with one arm." Al deftly pulled the knife through one of the thick slices of bread, making it two.

"I don't think I'll enjoy the preacher's company for a two-day trip."

Cora's eyes grew wide. The reverend was good company for Luke to keep. "You might be pleasantly surprised. He's a very educated man."

With his eyebrows lifted high on his forehead, Luke's expression told them all he was skeptical the reverend was the company he should keep.

Bertha set a platter of meat on the table. "Cora, would you get the pickled beets and the pitcher of water?" Bertha brushed past her and retrieved the plates and forks.

Cora obliged. She stepped from the pantry in time to see Luke shrug his shoulder. "Okay, but while I'm gone—" he pointed to Al "—you need to do a little tracking."

"Tracking?" Cora set a crock and pitcher on the table before she slipped onto the only empty chair, which was right beside Luke.

"Well, I don't mean to scare you, ladies. I think there's some underhandedness going on."

"What do you mean?" Cora jerked her head toward Luke.

"I took a ride to your former neighbors' homestead today. On the way back, I rode along the rocky crags at the edge of your property. I saw Clement's hired hand, the one with the lantern attached to his saddle, dressing out two bucks."

"What's so unusual about butchering game?"

Luke gave Bertha a pointed look. "Mule deer."

"You think they corralled those two deer and turned

them loose in the field to fight." The words rolled from Cora. "You think Clement sabotaged the neighboring homesteads?"

Icy chills crawled through her, as she remembered Clement's last visit to their homestead. How he surveyed their farmyard, noting all the improvements they'd made. She caught the slight nod of Al's head.

Luke cleared his throat. "We do. One morning in early spring I saw a faint light moving around the rock formations where your sheep wintered. I suspect you lost some of your flock to predators—not the four-legged variety, but the two-legged."

Cora's hard intake of breath vibrated in the back of her throat. Her high-pitched squeak echoed through the room. This information made all her suspicions about Clement fact.

"Clement wants our land, too, doesn't he?" Bertha placed a hand on her chest.

Luke and Al didn't have to put voice to their answers— the look they exchanged told Cora everything she needed to know. Hank had been right: Clement wasn't to be trusted. Cora let her eyes roam over her cozy house. Her gaze settled on the fireplace Hank had lovingly built with stones found on their land. He had said the hearth was the heart of the home. Anger blazed through her stronger than any fire that had ever burned in the hearth.

This was her home. No one was taking it from her. She looked at Bertha. "He's not taking our home."

Bertha gave her head a curt nod.

"Ladies, you need to be alert to danger." Luke's voice held an edge, a warning.

"We will." Bertha nodded. "We will take every precaution to keep our crop and herd safe."

"I don't know if you need to worry about your crop,

since I saw the slaughtered deer." Luke worried the edge
of his moustache with two fingers.

"What?"

Pain crossed through Luke's eyes. His lips turned down
into a deep frown. "I don't think Clement will use the same
means to get your homestead. It might not be your crop or
your herd you need to worry about. It might be..."

Cora's eyes widened. She put a hand to her chest. "Me."

Securing her hat with a long pearl-ended pin, Cora lifted
Henry to her hip. "Ready?"

Bertha nodded. She slipped the wire handle of an egg
basket on her arm and walked out the door.

Cora followed her mother-in-law, closing the door tight.
She stood on the porch, letting her eyes adjust to the late-
July sun.

She scanned her farmyard for signs of change.

The chickens roosted in the shade of the coop. Luke's
horse stood in the stall, stretching its neck toward the open
barn door. The door to the sod house was closed tight.
Nothing out of the ordinary. She'd counted her sheep after
filling their trough with fresh water. All twenty-five remained in the pen.

Breathing a sigh of relief, she stepped down off the
porch. Silence surrounded the women while they walked
along the dirt path toward Faith. Henry cooed, touching
the buttons of Cora's white blouse with the high lace collar.

What a novelty! A town, a mile from their homestead,
stood on land where less than three months ago had been
a vast prairie.

"Do you think Luke and Reverend Beacom made it to
Dunnebeck yet?" Bertha looked straight ahead, her voice
held a tense edge.

Since Luke's lunchtime warning yesterday, the happiness that had brightened Bertha's face in the last few weeks gradually faded, replaced with the pucker of worry.

"I guess it depends on how long they slept on the way. It was a mighty good idea you had to pack their meals. I'm sure they both appreciated it." Cora turned to Bertha and managed a weak smile.

"Harrumph." Bertha continued to stare off into the horizon.

Worry saturated Cora's heart, weighed it down the way a wet quilt made a clothesline sag. Bertha lost faith easily. Luke had no faith. Did she put too much hope in the Lord?

Impossible, He did everything for the good of His children. Cora breathed deeply, letting the fresh air cleanse her mind and spirit.

She turned her eyes to the vast expanse of blue sky. *Heavenly Father, look down upon your servants. Keep Luke and Reverend Beacom safe on their journey. Lift the worry and fear from Bertha and my hearts. Help us to trust in You during good times and bad. Amen.*

Halfway to town, the clip-clop of a horse's hooves sounded behind them. Cora turned. Her heart began to beat in double time. Clement and one of his hired hands rode up behind them.

"Good day, ladies." He tipped his hat. He lips turned up into a nasty smile when his eyes rested on Cora. Her skin prickled.

"Clement." Bertha greeted him and continued walking with her eyes focused on the horizon.

"Heading to town for another moneymaking venture?"

Walking faster, Cora screwed her face into a deep scowl. "What?"

"Selling eggs." Clement tipped his head toward Bertha's basket and chuckled.

"We aren't selling the eggs. Luke and Al are expecting

our delivery." Cora hoped Clement caught her inference that someone in Faith expected them. It might discourage Clement from continuing to ride beside them on their walk to town.

"Luke went to Dunnebeck. He left last night." Clement's words snapped out and a vicious sneer curled his lips.

Cora's heart pounded harder in her chest. How did Clement know their every move? What Luke suspected was right. She and her homestead were in danger.

He veered his horse toward her. She sidestepped, bumping into Bertha. She kept her eyes locked on Clement, trying to anticipate his next move.

"Now would be a good time for us to announce our engagement. The preacher can marry us upon his return. Although I must say I don't approve of the company he keeps. He's young, though. As a prominent member of the community, I'm going to have a stern talk with the preacher."

Although the horse didn't touch Cora, the warmth it generated flushed her face. The acrid smell of the sun heating up its flesh assaulted her nostrils. Faith was in view. Cora looped her arm through Bertha's and walked even faster.

Clement nodded his head at his hired hand who guided his horse to the other side of Bertha, sandwiching the woman between their steeds.

Cora looked at Bertha. Sweat beaded her brow and trickled down the sides of her face. Fear iced over the sparkle in her blue eyes. If they walked any faster, they'd be running. The edge of town was close, yet so far away.

Cora prayed that someone, anyone, from town would witness Clement's actions.

"Today's a perfect summer day, bright sunshine, warm breeze. Couldn't find a better day to announce our plans to marry. Where shall we announce it? The middle of Main Street?"

"No." Cora stopped. Bertha stumbled a little and rattled the eggs in her basket.

Clement's attempt to instill fear in her and Bertha was working, but not enough to make her submit to a lifetime of misery.

Her shout scared Henry. His wails echoed through the prairie.

"I am never going to marry you! Never! And you aren't going to get our homestead. I know you're the one behind all the destruction."

Taking a deep breath, Clement seemed to grow in his saddle. Menace glowed from his eyes. "I mean to have your land and the clear water in your well. One way or the other your homestead will be mine. If you want to stay on it, you'll marry me." His clipped words, spoken through clenched teeth, were low and threatening.

"Hey, what's going on over there?"

Cora saw surprise jerk Clement's body. He cranked his neck from side to side. She rose to her tiptoes to peer over the hired hand's horse. A railroad man stood behind a surveying device. God had answered her prayers—someone had seen them.

"Just talking to my neighbors." Clement's voice held a friendly lilt.

Before Cora could disagree, Clement jerked his head toward his hand who took off in the direction of Clement's ranch. Then Clement tipped his hat.

"Enjoy your day in town, ladies." Again, his voice held an airy tone for the sake of the railroad worker. He leaned down, placing his hat on his head. "You'll be sorry, Cora Anderson." He spurred his horse, riding toward Faith.

Cora bounced Henry, whose tears had soaked the shoulder of her cotton blouse. "There, there." She patted his back.

"M...m...maybe you should reconsider." Fear shook Bertha's voice.

She looked at her mother-in-law. "I'm not marrying Clement. He's an evil man."

Henry's wails subsided to a whimper. Cora wiped away his tears with her fingertips.

A tear ran down Bertha's cheek. "We're going to be homeless if you don't."

"No, we're not." Cora swiped the moisture from Bertha's cheek. "That happened to me once when my parents died and it's never going to happen to me again."

Cora looked out at the town lying on the horizon before them and started walking. "We need to keep our faith strong." She started to hum a hymn.

By the time they reached the outskirts of Faith, stubborn determination replaced all the fear that had surfaced with Clement's threat. Back ramrod-straight and head held high, Cora marched down the street to Al and Luke's plot.

"This town needs a marshal." Cora stepped onto the prepared site where Luke's hotel would sit and began to pace, her boots creating clouds of powdered dust with each abrupt turn.

"Good morning?" Al's voice rose a few octaves on the last word.

"I need a chair."

Cora looked up to see Al slide the straight-back chair he used for clients under Bertha. He relieved her of her basket.

"Clement threatened us." Bertha's words rushed from her. "Cora's going to have to marry him. There is no other way." She covered her face with her hands.

"What happened?" Al squatted before Bertha's chair. He covered her hands with his, pulling her palms from her face.

"Clement wanted to announce their engagement today.

Cora shouted at him. She said she'd never marry him and then he said..."

"What? What did he say?"

Bertha shook her head.

"He said—" Cora walked over to them "—our homestead with the clear water would be his one way or the other."

"Well, Reverend Beacom's brother is a U.S. marshal. He's going to telegraph him while they are in Dunnebeck to see what it takes to get law in town."

"Really?" Hope brightened Bertha's face.

Al nodded.

The jangle of a buckboard stopping drew their attention to the street. Clement and his hired man jumped down from the seat.

"Cora Anderson, your sheep are diseased." Clement hollered his accusation so everyone within earshot heard. Hammering stopped. People on the street gathered around the wagon.

Pushing through the small crowd, Cora, Al and Bertha peered over the wagon side. A sheep lay on its side. Eyes closed, it appeared to be sleeping.

"My sheep are not diseased."

"How do you explain this?" Clement made a dramatic sweep of his arm over the wagon. "You are the only homesteader with unshorn sheep. I think it's hoof and mouth. Get your guns. The whole herd should be killed before our cattle are infected."

Handing Henry to Bertha, Cora reached over the side of the wagon and stuck her fingers into the wool. What met her fingertips was startling. She turned to Al. "It's still warm."

In a quick move, he jumped into the wagon bed. He ran his fingers through the wool, stopping at the neckline. Answering the signal of his head jerk, Cora looked at the wool around the sheep's neck. It'd been fluffed out. She pushed her fingers through the tight fibers around the sheep's neck. The inner wool close to the sheep's skin was matted and separated about the width of her finger or a rope.

"It's been strangled." Horrified, she turned to Clement. "You strangled one of my sheep."

Fire blazed in his eyes. "I did not. Your animals are diseased."

Al stood tall in the wagon. "Folks, he's lying. This sheep shows no signs of infection. Take a good look."

The men standing around looked over the animal.

"Is this what he was bothering you about on your way to town, ma'am?" The railroad worker who'd been surveying stepped forward, eyeing Clement suspiciously.

"Yes, it is. He wants my homestead." The words tumbled from Cora before she thought of the consequences they might bring.

Clement glowered at Cora.

"If you killed one of her sheep, I'd say it's punishable by law." The railroad worker crossed his arms over his chest.

Al jumped down from the wagon. "Yes, I believe it is."

The people who gathered at the wagon suddenly surrounded Cora. Had Clement's hired hand gone to her homestead and killed one of her sheep after Clement and his men had confronted her and Bertha?

Clement stepped back, palms up. "Perhaps, my hired man here was mistaken. I never took any of Mrs. Anderson's sheep. Surely, you believe an upstanding community leader?"

Several snorts and harrumphs sounded from the crowd, making Cora realize most folks weren't fond of Clement. Judging by the astonished look on his face, this was a surprise to him, too.

"Do you know how many head you have?" His fake smile didn't hide the hatred glowing in his eyes.

"Of course, I know how many head of sheep I have. Twenty-five."

"Perhaps you should go home and count them to prove our innocence. Neither I nor my hired hand stole or killed your sheep."

"No, you stay here, Mrs. Anderson. I'll go." The crowd parted so the railroad worker could get through.

Cora crossed her arms and met Clement's icy stare. "If I were you, I wouldn't go any farther than the office of your lumber business."

# Chapter 14

Frantic, Luke slapped the reins against Dutch.

"Slow down." Al called from the back of the wagon.

White-knuckled, Reverend Beacom held on to the buckboard seat and braced his feet against the wagon floor.

The lumber in the buckboard's box bounced and clacked with each bump the wagon wheels hit in the worn path to Cora's house.

Luke and Reverend Beacom had made good time on their trip, their mood jovial when they returned to Faith with the pristine and affordable lumber. Luke figured by working long days, they could build the hotel in less than a month once they laid the foundation. But Al met them before they had even dismounted from the wagon, relaying the stunt Clement had pulled on Cora late yesterday. Rage fisted Luke's hands, goading him to find Clement and give him a poke in the nose, but something stronger pushed his rage from his heart. Luke's anger at Clement was no match for the desire to see his loved ones. He wanted—no, needed—to touch them and know they were safe.

Al seemed to read his mind because he hopped into the wagon bed seconds before Luke whipped the reins against Dutch's hindquarters, sending him into a gallop toward home.

"I told you they were okay," Al shouted above the din of the jostling boards and Dutch's heavy hoofbeats.

Halfway to the homestead, Luke saw a narrow line of smoke curling up into the air. They were heating their wash water in the kettle above the rock fire pit. His eyes saw proof of what Al said was true, yet he didn't slow the wagon. His heart longed to see them all. Hold them in his arms. Soak up their warmth.

He flicked the reins, slapping the leather against Dutch's side. His wrist throbbed with each bump in the road. He gritted his teeth and bore it. He had to see his loved ones.

Reverend Beacom mumbled beside him, no doubt praying for his safety while Dutch's hoofs gobbled up the dirt, engulfing them in a dust cloud.

"Whoa." Luke commanded and pulled hard on the reins to slow Dutch at the edge of the farmyard. The horse snorted, slowed and finally stopped inches from the clotheslines. The commotion started the chickens flapping and cackling. Bertha and Cora rushed from the sod house, wiping their hands on their aprons.

Dropping the reins, Luke jumped from the wagon and ran to Cora. He wrapped his good arm around her, sealing her to him. Burying his face in her soft curls, he breathed deeply. The faint smell of lye scented her hair.

"I shouldn't have left you alone." He croaked, his voice hoarse with emotion.

"Luke." Cora wrapped an arm around his waist,

squeezing hard before gently pushing on his chest with her free hand.

Releasing her enough to look down on her loveliness, he searched her face. "Please forgive me. I should have been here to protect you. Where's Henry?"

Her beautiful pink lips turned into a smile. She lifted her hand to his cheek. "We're fine. He's in the house napping."

"I shouldn't have left you alone." He looked around, searching for Bertha. She stood beside Al while he unharnessed Dutch. She didn't look any the worse for wear.

"The herd?" With quick steps, Luke started walking with Cora still by his side. She stumbled over his boots. He flexed his arm to help her regain her balance and slowed down to a normal stride.

"They are fine." She tried to pull free from his embrace. He held tight and continued his walk to the pen.

"We've counted them three times since yesterday. All twenty-five of the sheep are safe and sound." Cora reassured him.

He did a silent count anyway. "Was the dead sheep one of yours?" Luke looked at Cora, drinking in the pretty face he knew he couldn't live without.

"I'm sure it's one of the many that went missing last spring. We chalked up the loss to coyotes." She shrugged. "Maybe Clement cut it from the herd and took it to his ranch. We are the only sheep farmers in this area."

He should have investigated on the cool spring morning when he saw the mysterious light. He was sure Clement had tried to thin her herd to discourage her from proving up.

*Her crop.* She couldn't prove up without it. "Did you check the sorghum?"

"Yes, the crop is fine. Both the sorghum and the gardens could use some rain. Other than that, the crops are intact."

His breath whooshed from his body. For the first time

since he'd hit Faith's main street and heard what happened, he really exhaled. The tension threading through him unraveled. His shoulders relaxed.

Loosening his hold on Cora, he turned her to face him. "All the way out here, I imagined the worst. I thought I'd lost my family."

Cora gasped softly and lifted her fingers to her mouth.

"Don't look so surprised, Cora. Surely, you know I love you."

Moisture dimmed her eyes. She nodded her head. "I love you, too."

The words he thought he never needed to hear swelled his heart with such joy he couldn't hold his happiness in, and he laughed. "I wish I had two working hands so I could lift you up and twirl you around." He clasped her hand and stared into her pretty green eyes. "Marry me, Cora."

She blinked several times and gave her head a slight shake. "You know I can't unless you become..." Her voice trailed off.

Disappointment gripped Luke's heart, stopping its merry pitter-patter. "A Christian." He snorted, released her hand and strode to the barn.

Luke leaned against an outer hotel wall, out of sight of the people gathered inside for Sunday services in the finished dining room.

It'd been a month since Clement had tried to ruin Cora's chances of proving up her homestead by convincing the townspeople her sheep were sick. Fresh anger filled him. It galled him that Clement had the nerve to cross the hotel's threshold to attend Sunday services.

Yet, Cora, Al and many other good people who planned to make Faith their home showed a different side of being Christian. They were charitable, forgiving and loving to their neighbors. The melody of a familiar hymn drifted out through the open window, lifting Luke's heart with its promising words of hope to those who believed in the Lord.

He'd stood in the shadows of his hotel, listening to Reverend Beacom's sermons since they made the trip to Dunnebeck together. The reverend made the Bible come to life and applied it to daily living.

He taught and *lived* the Word in the way the Bible instructed. He spoke of God's love and mercy for His children, instead of punishment and eternal damnation. That was a God Luke could believe in, not the one his dad preached about while pounding his fists on the pulpit in church and on Luke at home.

Something shifted in his heart and mind. Luke knew his father blamed him for his mother dying in childbirth. He'd heard and felt his father's rage many times. Now Luke could see his father was also angry with God. His father hadn't trusted God enough to give Him his burdens or allow Him to comfort his heart. Instead he let his grief and bitterness fester until he couldn't love anyone, not even God or Luke. His father preached the Word, but lacked faith, then he broke Luke's spirit until he lost all his faith, too.

Peace filled Luke's chest. He had faith, faith enough to leave his old life and work hard in search of a new one. A new life that he'd found in Faith, South Dakota. He smiled at the irony of his newfound feelings and the name of the town. Not only did he have a chance at a profitable business, he'd found something better—friends and a family.

Though the family part wasn't official, he knew it soon would be. He felt the movement in his heart. Cora would no longer have to worry about being yoked with an unbeliever.

"Please join me in the Lord's Prayer."

Luke's heart answered Reverend Beacom's gentle instruction. He bowed his head and did more than say the words. He felt them. He meant them.

When the service ended, Luke pushed off the side of the building and rounded the corner.

Some of the congregation bustled from the building, forming small groups in the grass to visit with their neighbors. Luke walked through the hotel door, nodding a greeting to the folks he passed.

Henry lay tummy down on a blanket. He pushed up with his hands, his eyes on his mother, who snapped a tablecloth through the air and let the starched lace float down on one of the round tables they'd pushed to the corner to make room for seating for the Sunday service.

Luke picked up two straight-back chairs from the two rows the congregants arranged for makeshift pews and carried them to the table where Bertha and Cora had set out food from their basket.

"Thank you." Cora's bright smile magnified her beauty. "And good morning."

"'Morning." Luke removed his hat and hung it over the spindle of one of the chairs. Cora wore the same gauzy dress she'd worn to the Independence Day ceremony. Her hat was adorned with a sprig of wild daisies. Her soft chestnut hair, braided and twirled into a bun at the base of her head, showed off her slender neck.

Luke looked down at his worn cotton trousers, muslin shirt and suspenders, wishing he'd put on his suit this morning.

Self-conscious, he bent his thumbs through the suspender's loops. "Could I help you with anything?"

"Yes, thank you. Do you mind getting your plates and silver?"

"Not at all." Luke's heavy footfalls echoed off the new wood floor with each step. He removed the plain white porcelain plates and cups from the kitchen shelving. He lifted the box of unadorned silver and tucked it under his left arm. His wrist had healed, but it was still weak and he didn't want to chance spilling the tableware on the floor.

Cora looked up when he reentered the room. His chest swelled with pride at the appreciation he saw in her eyes. He walked toward her. As he drew close to Cora, he saw the slight pucker of her lips. She gave her head a small shake. The glow in her eyes changed from love to friendliness.

"I'll take that." She slipped the box from under his arm. "What a treat it is to eat off china."

"It's not china." Luke had planned on delicate china, decorated with flowers and silver with etched handles to serve meals to his guests. He'd wanted his hotel to be a jewel on the prairie. Clement's underhandedness with the lumber reduced his savings, leaving him only enough for the scant necessities, simple and unadorned beds, tables and chairs. Once he turned a profit, though, he planned to change all the simple furnishings to the ornate ones in his original plan.

"Well, it's a treat for us. We sold our china before we came out to the homestead. Hank promised we'd buy another set when we settled. The enamel made more sense for the trip west and met our daily needs." A deep sigh escaped her. "I guess it still does."

Cora's answer brought a smile to Luke's lips. She was a Godly woman and took today's sermon to heart by being content with what she had. He reflected on his earlier thought. Not one customer had complained about his place settings or furniture. Was there really a need to replace them?

A mason jar filled with clear water sat in the center of the table, a platter of fried chicken, a large bowl of potato salad, pickled vegetables and bread circled it like the pump standing erect in the center of Cora's farmyard surrounded by outbuildings.

"Quite a spread."

"There is chocolate cake for dessert. Sunday dinners are special." As soon as her words were out, Cora's expression turned wary.

Luke smiled. "Yes, I know."

"Most of it is from the sweat of our brow, which Bertha and I couldn't have done without Al and your help. We've filled two pantries with our canning and have plenty to spare. Bertha, Al and I discussed our abundance. We'd like to give some to Reverend Beacom." Wariness filtered through Cora's words. She lifted her brows, turning her statement into a question.

"Then why haven't you?" Luke stifled a chuckle at the disbelief in Cora's expression. She obviously thought an argument would ensue and, to be honest, a few weeks ago one would have. Luke knew the people in town didn't have money to spare so the offerings in the weekly plate must be meager and Reverend Beacom had to eat.

Cora recovered from her shock, her eyes twinkling with delight. "We will get a box to him the next time we come to town."

Clement's booming laugh drifted in through the window. The shine in Cora's eyes dimmed.

"I have a little over a month to prove up my homestead. Do you think we'll make it?" Fear filled her voice and eyes.

Clement hadn't bothered Cora since the hot July day. Luke's gut told him Clement was lying low due the towns-folks' public support of Cora. Letting time pass gave people time to forget and built false hope in Cora, leading her to believe she'd prove up her homestead.

"I think you need to be on your guard until the day the deed is yours." Disappointment wilted her stance the way the hot summer sun drooped the wildflowers. Luke's heart wilted, too, dipping down in his chest because he couldn't give her the reassurance she'd sought. She needed to stay alert to any danger. Evil underlay all of Clement's actions, even if he did try to hide under his public image.

Al and Bertha joined them at the table. "Is something wrong?"

Luke tipped his head toward the window where Clement's loud voice carried through the yard.

"He's still trying to make nice with many of the business owners." Al held out a chair and after Bertha slipped onto it, he helped her scoot under the table.

Cora primly stood by her chair, eyes riveted to the floor.

"Let me help you." Luke mirrored Al's manners.

Al sat between the two women. "When they found out the price we paid for our lumber in Dunnebeck, it confirmed he took advantage of the situation, charging double for poor-quality wood."

Folding his frame onto the other chair, Luke nodded his head in agreement.

"Let's not spoil our dinner talking about Clement." Bertha, dressed in a butter-yellow cotton dress with a lace yoke and pearl buttons, unfolded a neatly pressed linen napkin and placed it on her lap. "Cora, you must stop and look at Al's new barber chair. Why it's padded and very comfortable to sit in."

Her face beamed with pride and love when she looked at Al. Luke longed to see the same expression in Cora's eyes. He saw brief glimpses of it before Cora reeled her emotions back in, fought her feelings.

She couldn't be yoked with an unbeliever. That had changed. She just didn't know it yet. Her faith was oaktree solid; his wavered like a sapling shoot in the wind. He still had questions he needed answered, but he did know God existed and He loved his children, including Luke.

## Chapter 15

Cora rearranged the crates in the wagon box to squeeze in the last basketful of laundry.

Bertha stood on the porch holding Henry. "Oh, good. The sun dried the ground up some. Our good skirts won't get soiled by the mud." She stepped from the porch with Henry nestled in the crook of her arm.

Cora stepped lightly around a muddy low spot in the yard and met Bertha at the side of the wagon.

The skies opened up the last week in August, saturating the ground and making it impossible to do laundry. Cora and Bertha made good use of the time, putting up corn and tomatoes, making pickles.

After the rain stopped, they immediately started washing and ironing their customers' baskets of clothing, bedding and towels. They worked from sunup to sundown to get their customers' washing caught up. Between the railroad men and Luke and Al's laundry, they were no longer able to walk to town with all the clean clothes.

Once Bertha was situated on the bench with Henry on her lap, Cora rounded the end of the wagon. She stopped and wiggled the crate that held full mason jars. Satisfied the glass jars were secure, she climbed up onto the bench seat.

Cora lifted the reins. "Giddyup."

The wagon jerked into motion and Cora hoped the wheels would make it through the mud on the path to town. Bertha sang to Henry, while Cora scanned the horizon for signs of trouble. She saw a rider heading in the direction of Clement's ranch. The increased tempo of her heartbeat pounded out its worry against her chest.

The man saw the wagon. Stopping his horse, he watched the women.

Cora recognized Clement's hired hand—the one who was afraid of the dark. *Dear God, don't let him turn toward us.*

He lifted an arm and gave them a friendly wave. Cora didn't return the greeting and he continued on his way.

"Maybe we should go back home," Bertha whispered, even though there was no one else around.

Cora considered her words. "We're almost to town. We'll make our deliveries and then return home. It shouldn't take us longer than an hour."

Out of the corner of her eye, she saw Bertha's shoulders sag. The picnic basket resting between their feet, filled with mulberry pie, would be left instead of shared with Al and Luke.

"I can drop you and Henry off at Luke's hotel so you can have a short visit with Al." The rain had kept the men in town, adding finishing touches to the hotel's interior.

A wide smile lit up Bertha's face. "Thank you. Are you sure? You'll miss out on a visit."

The rattle of Cora's inhale cut through the flatlands. She needed to avoid visiting Luke. The more she saw him, the harder it was to tamp down her feelings and to remember God's instructions. "I'm sure."

She kept her words light, fighting to keep her own shoulders from sagging. Even though she couldn't act on her feelings, she'd missed seeing Luke the past week.

Cora guided Dutch around the deep ruts running through Main Street. She stopped in front of the hotel.

"Oh, look." Bertha turned to Cora. "The barber pole is up. Looks official, doesn't it?"

The red, white and blue porcelain pole resembled a large, striped candy stick. The men had mounted it right beside the front door of the hotel, giving the rough wood a splash of color.

"Yes, it does. It looks very nice."

Al happened to be looking out the window in the small parlor housing his barbershop and rushed through the door. He called over his shoulder. "Luke, they made it to town."

He unburdened Henry from Bertha's arms then held her hand while she dismounted. The soft dirt squished when her boot hit the ground.

Luke strode through the door, pulling on the straps of his suspenders, his hat askew on his head. "Good afternoon, ladies. Can I help you with anything?"

"Your laundry is in that basket." Cora turned in her seat and pointed. "This one belongs to Al and your share of the garden produce is in the apple crate."

Al handed Henry to Bertha and lifted his basket from the wagon bed. Luke had his basket under one arm and the small crate under the other. Cora handed Bertha the pie.

"Aren't you staying?" Luke's mouth turned into a sad pout.

Closing her eyes, Cora steeled her resolve. Luke knew

what he had to do if he wanted to spend time with her. "I have deliveries to make." She clicked her tongue and headed down the street so she could deliver to the railroad men.

She pulled the wagon close to the building's platform. The men stopped their work and came over to collect their washing. Cora stepped onto the platform. From the raised level she noticed a rider crossing the prairie at a gallop. He reached town and turned down Main Street. As Cora looked across the horizon, a faint swirl of smoke twisted into the sky. She turned her attention back to the railroad men collecting their clothes and paying their debts.

As she put the last of their money into her purse, someone shouted her name.

"Cora!"

She jerked her head up and saw Luke rounding the corner of a building, his horse at a gallop.

"Your house."

The urgency in his voice set off alarms. *The smoke*. She looked in the direction of the homestead. The small swirl had turned into ugly black clouds of billowing smoke darkening the blue sky.

Luke stopped his horse beside the wagon. "Let's go."

She started to sit.

"Leave the wagon. It's too cumbersome." Luke reached out his hand.

Cora grasped it and in one fluid movement, Luke pulled her into a sidesaddle position between him and the saddle horn.

"Hold on."

She grabbed a hunk of the horse's coarse mane at the same time Luke spurred him into a gallop. "How do you know it's my house?"

Luke's breath heaved from him. "A railroad surveyor

saw the smoke and went to investigate. He tried to douse the flames and thought he got the fire put out, but..."

His voice trailed off. Cora saw other riders dotting the prairie, their shapes blurred by her tears. How did this happen? They hadn't stirred the embers in the cookstore since early in the morning so it couldn't be from a wayward spark.

She thought of Clement's hired hand. Had he been watching, waiting for them to leave? Angry sobs burned the back of her throat. Had he doubled around and started their house on fire?

"Can you go any faster?" Cora shouted, even though she knew the answer. The water-soaked ground sucked at the horse's hooves, slowing its progress.

"Don't worry. A railroad man rode through town hollering 'fire.' Most of the townsfolks dropped what they were doing and headed out to help." His words were meant to comfort her, but they dripped with worry of his own.

Even from a distance, the acrid fumes of the smoke seared Cora's nostrils. The burnt aroma settled in her mouth, gagging her. The dark smoke lifted and spread in the sky, mocking her dreams of having a home.

They reached the edge of the farmyard. The men formed a human chain from the pump to the house, passing buckets from man to man. Heaviness grew in her chest and pressed down until she thought she'd cave under the pressure.

Her stomach lurched, and she felt like she was about to retch. The west side of the house, where the stone fireplace was built, smoldered with thick black smoke. The flames hissed their displeasure with each douse of a bucket.

Luke slowed and guided his horse away from the frenzy. Cora slid from the saddle and hit the ground running. Smoke engulfed her, choking the air from her lungs. The intense heat forced her to narrow her eyes to mere slits and run half-blind toward the house.

The ground seemed to fall away. She took longer strides. Her legs pumped, yet she didn't get closer to the house. It took a few seconds for her to realize her feet were flailing in the air. Strong arms circled her waist and lifted her off the ground.

"You can't go in. It's dangerous." Luke's tone was sharp and scolding.

Cora struggled against his hold with all her might. "My house!"

"I know." Luke breathed the words into her ear. Setting her on the ground, he turned her to face him. Running his hand down the length of her hair, he rested it on her cheek. "I know."

His compassion-filled eyes were hazed with a thin layer of moisture.

Hot tears burned her eyes. "What are we going to do?" She buried her head in his neck and sobbed.

The shouts of the men, the click of the iron pump handle, and the clip-clop of horses' hooves became a muffled backdrop while her mind tried to comprehend the loss of her homestead. She followed Luke's gentle tug. She walked with him away from the house. A cool breeze refreshed her heated skin.

"I came as soon as I heard."

The voice loud and clear, drew Cora ramrod-straight. She shoved away from Luke and turned to Clement. "You did this." She took a step toward him. "You burned my house down." Another step closed the space between them. Grief and anger changed her petite stature, making her feel taller, stronger. "You are not getting my homestead."

She surprised herself with the force of her words. Clement's eyes grew wide, then narrowed. "Why Mrs. Anderson,

I have witnesses that I was at the lumberyard all morning. How could I have set fire to your home?"

His arrogant chuckle spurred Cora's anger into rage. She pounced. Hands fisted, she beat his chest. "I saw your hired man this morning. He doubled back and set my house on fire. We haven't had a fire in the hearth since February." Her voice turned shrill and icy, mirroring Clement's. "You're not getting my homestead. I'll die before you do."

Clement's pudgy fingers sank into her upper arms, pinching hard before he pushed her away. Clement lifted his palm and pulled back to slap her in the face. "You must have a left a hot ember in the hearth."

Before she could take a breath or brace for the impact of his hand, Luke stood between them. His right fist connected with Clement's jaw. Clement staggered back a few steps and wobbled before regaining his balance. When he opened his eyes, they shone with an evil so dark, Cora's skin prickled. He'd kill her if he had to in order to own her land.

With hate-filled eyes, Clement stalked to his horse. "I came by to offer to sell you lumber at half price so you could rebuild, have a house to live in and a chance to save your homestead." He shouted the words so all the people in the farmyard could hear.

"Cora, Bertha and Henry can stay in the hotel until they figure out what to do." Luke still stood between Cora and Clement.

"Splendid idea. I guess I'll change my offer. Instead of selling you lumber, I'll buy your homestead." Clement leaned over his saddle horn, wiping the blood from his swelling lip with the back of his hand. "The rules of proving up say you have to live on the land and by the looks of your house with its missing wall and you taking up residence in the hotel, you don't meet the criteria."

Pushing past Luke, Cora shouted, "I will never sell my land to you."

A snide smile played at Clement's lips. "You don't have to. The land office will."

Cora watched Clement ride away.

"He's not taking my homestead. I'm staying in the sod house." Cora turned on her heel and marched past Luke. He caught her arm.

"No, you aren't. It's too dangerous."

"I have to save my home." Cora jerked her arm in an attempt to free herself from Luke's grip.

Luke tightened his hold. "Cora." He turned her to face him. "You aren't staying out here. Clement is a dangerous man."

Cora narrowed her eyes. "I am saving my home. I won't be homeless again."

"You can't risk your life for this land."

"Henry needs a home."

"No, Henry needs a *mother*. Don't let him grow up without one. I know how that feels. *You* are more important to him than a house."

A small sob choked out of her. "I failed my father and lost his farm. I can't fail Hank the same way."

"You won't." Luke pulled her into a tight hug. "We'll go to the hotel and figure this out."

"The entire west wall is gone. The stone foundation of the fireplace is caved in." Cora held Bertha's hands in hers, both of them letting their tears flow freely. Henry dozed in the middle of a brass feather bed in an upstairs room of the hotel.

"What are we going to do?" Bertha whispered.

"You need to stay here with Henry. I'm going back and

living in the sod house. Clement is not going to take our homestead away from us."

"Don't do it. It's too dangerous."

"It's the only thing we can do. I have less than a month to prove up and I fully intend to." Determination filled her voice. "Many people prove up their claims living in a sod house."

"That's not what I mean. If someone set our house on fire, they might try to harm you. Besides, it will only be a night or two. All the town men said they'd help Luke and Al rebuild the wall when Reverend Beacom comes back from Dunnebeck with the lumber."

"It's a risk I have to take. Clement will get word to the land office. They'll check and if I'm not living there, I'll lose the homestead with only three weeks left to prove up. Besides, I will only be alone during the night. The sod house has a reinforced door. I'll be fine."

Bertha rubbed her forehead. "This is not a good idea." Bertha pulled Cora into a tight hug. "I understand, though, and won't stop you. Be careful, daughter, I couldn't bear to lose you."

Touched, moisture brimmed in Cora's eyes. "It will be okay. I'll slip out quietly."

Wiggling to free herself from Bertha's embrace, Cora walked to the bed where Henry slept. Lightly, she brushed her knuckles against his cheek. She wasn't going to let him down.

"Let Luke go with you."

"No, it's not proper."

"I'm not worried about proper. I'm worried about you."

Cora shook her head and gave Bertha a small smile. Taking one last look at Henry, she gingerly walked through the hotel room door.

She peered over the banister. No sign of Luke. The new

wood of the stairs groaned under her weight. She made it to the bottom without drawing notice. She peeked around the door of the barbershop. Al's back was turned away from the opening while he shaved a customer.

Stealing past his door undetected, she ran to the road and around the corner to the path out of town before her doubts and fears could turn her around. She walked quickly, keeping aware of her surroundings. She didn't want to meet Clement or his hired hand on the path.

Fear iced her blood. She craned her neck, scanning the area and walked faster. He'd already done enough damage to her home and was confident he'd buy it out from under her; he'd surely leave it alone now.

The lingering aroma of smoke and wet ashes assaulted her, stinging her eyes and nose when she stepped into her farmyard. She stopped for a moment and grieved the damage to the outside of the house. Steeling herself to see the damage on the inside, she walked straight to the door of the house.

Cora opened the door and stepped across the threshold. She walked to the center of the room, leaving a path of sooty footprints.

The bright green curtains over the window were dingy with ash and singed around the edges. Her hand-stitched quilt, a wedding gift from Bertha, was blackened and smoke-stained. All of these items could be cleaned or replaced, but not the fireplace. There was no saving the fireplace.

Sighing, Cora started to strip her feather mattress so she could carry it to the sod house. Once the task was done, she went to the pantry to get new bedding, certain the soot had filtered through the burlap curtain and soiled it, too. As she lifted the sheets from the shelf and shook them, a thin layer of black soot snowed down onto the floor. She slipped through the burlap curtain, but movement by the window caught her eye. Placing the bedding on the table, she crept to the window.

Cora kept her body in the shadows and peered out the smoke-fogged glass. Clement walked through her farmyard, bobbing back and forth under the weight of the two buckets he carried. She surveyed the landscape of her ranch. She didn't see a horse or a wagon. On tiptoes she silently walked to the small back window by the cookstove. Clement had tethered his horse to the fence post of the sheep pen. A shovel leaned on the cross boards of her fence.

She frowned. She didn't remember leaving the shovel there. Perhaps Luke, Al or one of the other men who helped put out the fire had. Cora turned from the window. The men may have used the shovel to dig a fire line, but why would they leave the shovel by the fence? It didn't make sense.

*The buckets!*

Racing to the window, Cora no longer worried about her footsteps on the wooden floor. Clement set the buckets on the ground beside the pump and started to pry the boards from the well. Stretching high on her toes, she tried to see what was in them. *No.* Not even Clement would be evil enough to stoop that low.

The crack of the first board coming off the base of the well opening confirmed her fear. Clement planned to dump manure down her well. If he succeeded her homestead would be worthless.

The thought spurred her into action. Cora ran from the house. *Please Lord, be with me. Help me to preserve the fresh water in our well and to save my home. Amen.*

"Stop!"

Clement's body jerked. The hammer claw slipped from the end of the board, flipping the hammer from his hand.

"What are you doing here? I thought you were living at the hotel."

Evil twisted Clement's features. Cora stopped short, throwing off her balance. She stumbled a little. Righting herself, she started to back away. "No, I'm living in the sod house so I can prove up my homestead." Fear shook her words.

"Harrumph. You are silly little fool. You should have married me." A funny gleam crossed through Clement's eyes. "You still could." He walked toward her. "If I soil you, you have no other choice and then I wouldn't have to taint your well. I'd have the best water in this territory and the most valuable land."

The rush of fear pounded in her ears. If she ran, she could save herself, but she'd lose her pure water and eventually her homestead. If she stayed...an icy chill coursed through her body, freezing her into place while Clement closed the gap between them, a sinister smile curling his lips.

*Lord, please help me.* Cora closed her eyes. A peaceful feeling washed through her, strengthening her faith. Reassured, she opened her eyes and smiled at Clement.

Luke rode along the dirt path leading to Cora's homestead, thankful Bertha's worries had overtaken her conscience and she had confessed Cora's plan to Al. Al immediately told Luke, who tied a bedroll to his saddle. Although it wasn't proper, Luke planned to stay in the barn while Cora slept in the sod house.

He shook his head. Cora was too headstrong for her own good, yet it was one of the qualities he loved about her. He couldn't wait to surprise her on Sunday when he walked into the church service and sat down beside her, Bertha, Henry and Al.

He looked up into the vast expanse of blue sky. He had given up on God, but God hadn't given up on him. He sent good, kind people to love him and bring him back to the fold.

When Luke reached the halfway point on the path to Cora's homestead, a large dark cloud covered the setting sun. Gloomy shadows seemed to crush down on him. His heart twisted.

*Cora!* A chilling sensation, similar to the one he'd felt on the long-ago spring day, overcame him. Something was wrong. This time he didn't need a voice to tell him to go. He spurred his horse.

"Dear Lord, keep her safe until I can get there. Amen." He shouted his prayer into the sky while leaning low in the saddle. The horse's hooves ate up the moist ground. Small mud balls pinged against Luke's trousers. In minutes, he arrived at the edge of the farmyard.

Luke reined his horse, jumping from the saddle before it came to a complete stop.

"Don't you touch her." Threat edged his voice. He ran between Cora and Clement.

"You aren't going to stop me this time. I've dug for clear water all over my homestead and there isn't one drop. This land is meant to be mine even if it comes with the price of a woman and a child." Clement lunged at Luke, fists flailing. "The land office refused to sell me this property. If I can't have the clear water, no one can."

Luke clenched his own fists, the stench of manure thick in his nose. He ducked before Clement's fist made contact with his jaw. The force of the missed punch caused Clement to stumble forward.

"Run." Luke shouted at Cora before turning his body.

Cora obeyed him. She ran, right past him and Clement. Luke turned. She hefted a bucket. "I'm not letting him dump manure down my well."

"Get on my horse and ride to safety."

Cora continued to drag the bucket away from the pump.

A growl alerted Luke to turn back to Clement who was on his feet. He came at Luke, his arms in the air like an angry bear stretched on two hind legs, ready to attack.

"Leave it and get to safety." Luke called over his shoulder again and watched Clement charge at him. A bucket rattled to the ground and Cora's skirts swished. Able to fully concentrate on Clement, Luke waited for the right moment and sidestepped in the way he'd learned to get away from his father's fists. He twirled around in time to see Clement's foot tromp down into a bucket.

Another growl filled the air. Clement lifted his foot and tried to shake the bucket from it. He jerked his head back and forth. "When I'm done with you." He looked at Luke. "She's next."

He kicked his leg hard. The bucket flew toward the house and Clement's weight-bearing leg slipped out from under him. The bucket Cora dropped had spilled its contents and mixed with the rain-soaked ground, making the area slick.

Clement's flapping arms were no match for his girth, and he fell backward. A hard thud and a ring of iron stopped Clement's threats.

Luke's breath came hard. Cora stood a few feet away. Their eyes met before they rushed to the pump and Clement's lifeless body.

Cora hid behind Luke, peeking over his shoulder. "Is he?" Her breath came hard and fast.

"He's alive, just knocked out." Luke pointed to the shallow movement of Clement's chest. "We need to tie him up."

"No, you don't." Luke turned and saw Reverend Beacom and a man who could be his twin, riding into the farmyard.

"This is my brother, Marshal Beacom. He'll take care of Clement."

"How did you know to come out here?" Luke reached for Cora, pulling her into the safety of his arms.

"Clement's hired hand was in the saloon shooting off his mouth." Reverend Beacom slipped down from his horse.

"Thank God."

"What did you say?" Cora pushed free enough to tilt her head and look up into his eyes.

"I said thank God Clement's hired hand has loose lips."

He tried to stifle his laugh, but the astonishment on her face tickled him to his core until his merriment bubbled from him.

Lifting her chin with his fingers, he touched his lips to hers then looked into her eyes. "Thank you, Cora for reminding me. God is good."

Clement groaned when the marshal turned him over to look at his head.

"It's men who are evil. Men, like Clement and my father, made me lose faith in the goodness of God. You, Al, Bertha and little Henry showed me how true believers act."

A single tear trickled down Cora's cheek, changing the course of its path at her upturned lips.

"I love you, Cora Anderson."

Her cheeks flamed red at his declaration of affection in front of the Beacom brothers, giving her quite a fetching glow.

Luke's laugh rang out. "I know it's not proper to say in front of others. I couldn't hold it in any longer."

Cora peeked over Luke's shoulder then rose up on tiptoes until her lips grazed his cheek. "I love you, too."

Her whisper flooded Luke's body with warmth and his heart with contentment.

"Marry me, Cora, and we'll get your homestead proved up."

Cora pulled back from his embrace. Her eyes narrowed before she arched a brow and smiled. "I'd be honored to be Mrs. Luke Dow, however we won't be proving up my homestead."

The shock of her words caused his smile to fade.

Her happy giggle bounced through the farmyard. Cora threw her arms around his neck. "We'll be proving up *our* homestead."

# Epilogue

"It's beautiful." The vapor of Cora's breathy whisper hung in the frigid December air.

This was her first glimpse of the Emmanuel chapel car. She'd never imagined a church on rails, but here it was parked on a spur track, a railroad car with a sanctuary on the inside, giving people in rural areas a church to worship in until they could build their own churches.

Evergreen boughs draped in scallops from window to window decorated the sides of the train car. Small wreaths of pine and holly covered the meeting points of the festive greenery. Additional fir branches twisted around the wrought-iron stair railing with a large wreath hanging over the center of the banister.

Oil lanterns glowed through the windows, showing the same type of decorations edging the ceiling inside. Many of the townspeople, decked out in their finery, sat in the wooden seats bolted to the floor that served as pews.

The seasonal decor was a perfect addition to their wedding. Love's warmth swirled through Cora, pushing away winter's chills from her nose.

Al reined Dutch to a stop a few feet from the chapel train car parked on the newly laid spur off the railroad track. He jumped from the wagon seat and hitched Dutch to a post.

Bertha grasped Cora's hand. The warmth of her touch radiated through their woolen mittens. Moisture brimmed in her blue eyes. Bertha had given Luke her blessing to court and marry Cora, but perhaps now that the hour of their marriage was near, Bertha's thoughts were on Hank, giving her a change of heart.

Cora squeezed Bertha's hand.

"You couldn't have found a finer man to raise my grandson. He loves him like he is his own kin. And he loves you, too."

Cora's heart swelled, her eyes threatened to spill her happiness down her cheeks. She blinked back her tears. Emotion clogged her throat so she smiled and nodded in agreement.

"Are you ready?" Al held his hand out to assist Bertha from the wagon seat. Once her feet were firmly planted on the frozen ground, Cora handed a tightly bundled Henry to Al. "I'll get them inside and settled, then come back and get you."

"Okay." Cora watched the couple walk arm in arm along the edge of the railroad tracks.

Cora's nerves tumbled through her, making it hard to sit still on the wagon seat. She drew a deep breath of the frosty air, thankful snow was scarce in western South Dakota this December. It made their trip to town easier. In a few minutes, she and Luke would be husband and wife.

Sitting in evening's twilight, the frigid air numbed her nose. All she needed was a red nose on her wedding day.

She pulled her wool scarf higher and watched a group of folks gather at the stairs of the chapel car, each waiting their turn to climb the wrought-iron stairs and enter the sanctuary.

"It's something, isn't it? A church on wheels."

Cora's heart began to race. She sat rigid on the wagon seat, resisting the urge to look at him. "What are you doing here?"

"Sneaking a peek at the lovely bride."

"Well, you shouldn't be."

Luke's soft chuckle sent a warm shiver swirling through her, flushing her face.

"You know it's tradition that the groom doesn't see the bride before the wedding." Cora fought the urge to turn around and look at her handsome husband-to-be.

"Don't worry. You have your back to me and you're bundled under all those quilts. I wasn't even sure it was you until you spoke."

His teasing brought a smile to her lips. "It's me, Cora Anderson."

"Soon to be Cora Dow."

Her smile widened. She'd practiced saying her new name in private for the last four months. "Are you sorry we waited?"

"No, I wanted to do this properly. You needed to honor Hank and finish mourning and we needed to officially court before we married."

Frozen grass crunched under Luke's footsteps. He was on her left, walking closer. Cora turned her face so he couldn't see his bride.

She looked at the railroad car. They'd planned to have their wedding in the hotel's dining room, until the train pulled the Emmanuel car to town. Then Reverend Beacom had made arrangements with the minister of the chapel car so that Cora and Luke could be married in a church.

"Yes. The men in town worked all afternoon hanging the evergreen boughs on the inside and outside of the train car. The ladies polished the mahogany walls and brass trim on the inside before taking over the dining room of the hotel and readying it for our wedding dinner."

"It's a wonderful town, isn't it?"

"It's more than a town." Frozen grass crunched as Luke took another step closer to the front of the wagon. "It's our home."

"Yes, it is and always will be. I have the documents from the land office to prove it." A bubble of pride puffed Cora's chest. After Clement's arrest and with the help of the townsfolk, a new wall was raised on her house. She'd proved up her land claim and after tonight, she'd need to change the names on the deed to her homestead.

"I wondered if that was you hiding in the shadows when we pulled up." Al took quick steps to the buckboard. "You shouldn't be out here, Luke. It goes against tradition."

"That's what I told him. We want to start our marriage out right."

A hearty laugh bounced through the stillness of the night. "We have all we need to begin our future together— love and faith."

Cora's heart filled with happiness and pride swelled her chest. Knowing Luke loved her was bliss, but his acceptance of the Lord filled her soul with joy. She longed to turn around and see his handsome face and the merriment that must be dancing there. Instead, she looked at Al, whose broad smile also showed his pride in Luke.

"Go on, now, so I can get the bride to the church on time."

At the first crunch of dry prairie grass, Cora closed her

eyes. Not because she believed the old wives' tale, but because she wanted her first glimpse of Luke on their wedding day to be standing at the altar, waiting for her. "Tell me when he's inside the chapel car."

A few seconds passed before she felt Al remove the quilt from her shoulders. "He's inside. Now it's your turn."

Cora gathered her skirt and carefully dismounted from the wagon. She slipped one mittened hand through Al's arm and carried her Bible in the other.

When they reached the iron stairs, Reverend Beacom and Bertha waited on the small platform. Cora climbed the stairs before removing her warm outer layers of clothing.

"Give me three minutes to put your things in the sleeper part of the car." Reverend Beacom, burdened with her and Al's coats, cracked opened the door to the chapel car and slid through.

A shiver shuddered through Cora, shaking her body. The bitter cold cut through the thin satin of her wedding gown. The ankle-length hem and long sleeves provided no protection from the cold. Her lace-gloved fingers stiffened around the Bible she'd carry instead of a bouquet while Bertha smoothed her hair back into place before attaching a lace veil to the crown of her head, making sure it covered the ringlets hanging down her back.

"Beautiful." Bertha stood back for a moment. "God certainly placed me in the middle of a perfect family and I hope to have more grandchildren to enjoy." Her blue eyes sparkled when she looked from Cora to Al. Bertha's dour expression had disappeared after she and Al were married in the fall. They temporarily lived in the sod house. Tomorrow they'd move into Luke's room in the hotel.

"Hurry on inside and get seated." Al patted his upper arms before he rubbed the chill from his hands. Even the coarse wool of his brown suit was no match for the north wind's kiss.

Bertha opened the door of the railroad car, then looked over her shoulder. "Cora, dear, put your best foot forward."

Once Bertha entered the Emmanuel train car, Al turned Cora to face him.

"I know that I'm no replacement for your father. But I am honored to give you away, Cora. You are the daughter I never had." He gently squeezed her arms.

Cora thought of her father and Hank. What a blessing they'd been in her life. Her eyes welled, but she smiled broadly. "Families change. It's only fitting my father-in-law gives me away."

Al opened the door of the chapel car. Cora stepped across the threshold. The paneled interior of the church car, polished to a high shine, reflected the light of the kerosene wall lanterns. Wicks trimmed low, the flames cast a soft candlelit hue in the long train car. Two large wreaths decorated the pulpit and the organ.

The din of the townsfolk hushed when they realized the bride had entered the chapel car, except for one loud voice.

"Dadadadadadada." Henry squealed and wiggled on Bertha's lap, stretching his arms to Luke.

Love surged through Cora. Luke would help her mold her son into a fine Christian man.

Reverend Beacom raised his arms. No one knew how to play the organ that was installed in the chapel car, so the congregation stood and began singing a hymn so Cora could march down the aisle.

Although the narrow aisle barely allowed two people to walk down it, Cora felt blessed to be married in this railroad sanctuary. If it wasn't for the railroad building a terminus and birthing a town, she wouldn't have met Luke and, more importantly, his faith might never have been restored.

Al patted her hand, which looped through his arm. Cora took a step, not worrying if she put her best foot forward. She'd done that many years ago when she accepted the Lord. She knew if you had faith and believed His word, He provided for His children. Cora had great faith that God would bless her and Luke with a long and wonderful life together, filled with love.

She lifted her eyes. Luke's soft and tender expression while he waited for her beside the pulpit chased away all of winter's chill from her skin, replacing it with excited tingles of their new, faith-filled life together.

\* \* \* \* \*

# REQUEST YOUR FREE BOOKS!

## 2 FREE INSPIRATIONAL NOVELS
## PLUS 2
# FREE
## MYSTERY GIFTS

*Love Inspired*®

**YES!** Please send me 2 FREE Love Inspired® novels and my 2 FREE mystery gifts (gifts are worth about $10). After receiving them, if I don't wish to receive any more books, I can return the shipping statement marked "cancel." If I don't cancel, I will receive 6 brand-new novels every month and be billed just $4.74 per book in the U.S. or $5.24 per book in Canada. That's a savings of at least 21% off the cover price. It's quite a bargain! Shipping and handling is just 50¢ per book in the U.S. and 75¢ per book in Canada.* I understand that accepting the 2 free books and gifts places me under no obligation to buy anything. I can always return a shipment and cancel at any time. Even if I never buy another book, the two free books and gifts are mine to keep forever.

105/305 IDN F49N

| Name | (PLEASE PRINT) | |
|------|------|------|

| Address | | Apt. # |
|------|------|------|

| City | State/Prov. | Zip/Postal Code |
|------|------|------|

Signature (if under 18, a parent or guardian must sign)

**Mail to the Harlequin® Reader Service:**
**IN U.S.A.:** P.O. Box 1867, Buffalo, NY 14240-1867
**IN CANADA:** P.O. Box 609, Fort Erie, Ontario L2A 5X3

**Are you a subscriber to Love Inspired books**
**and want to receive the larger-print edition?**
**Call 1-800-873-8635 or visit www.ReaderService.com.**

* Terms and prices subject to change without notice. Prices do not include applicable taxes. Sales tax applicable in N.Y. Canadian residents will be charged applicable taxes. Offer not valid in Quebec. This offer is limited to one order per household. Not valid for current subscribers to Love Inspired books. All orders subject to credit approval. Credit or debit balances in a customer's account(s) may be offset by any other outstanding balance owed by or to the customer. Please allow 4 to 6 weeks for delivery. Offer available while quantities last.

**Your Privacy**—The Harlequin® Reader Service is committed to protecting your privacy. Our Privacy Policy is available online at www.ReaderService.com or upon request from the Harlequin Reader Service.
We make a portion of our mailing list available to reputable third parties that offer products we believe may interest you. If you prefer that we not exchange your name with third parties, or if you wish to clarify or modify your communication preferences, please visit us at www.ReaderService.com/consumerschoice or write to us at Harlequin Reader Service Preference Service, P.O. Box 9062, Buffalo, NY 14269. Include your complete name and address.

LIDIR13R

# REQUEST YOUR FREE BOOKS!

## 2 FREE INSPIRATIONAL NOVELS
## PLUS 2
## FREE
## MYSTERY GIFTS

*Love Inspired*
# HISTORICAL
### INSPIRATIONAL HISTORICAL ROMANCE

**YES!** Please send me 2 FREE Love Inspired® Historical novels and my 2 FREE mystery gifts (gifts are worth about $10). After receiving them, if I don't wish to receive any more books, I can return the shipping statement marked "cancel." If I don't cancel, I will receive 4 brand-new novels every month and be billed just $4.74 per book in the U.S. or $5.24 per book in Canada. That's a savings of at least 21% off the cover price. It's quite a bargain! Shipping and handling is just 50¢ per book in the U.S. and 75¢ per book in Canada.* I understand that accepting the 2 free books and gifts places me under no obligation to buy anything. I can always return a shipment and cancel at any time. Even if I never buy another book, the two free books and gifts are mine to keep forever.

102/302 IDN F5CY

| | |
|---|---|
| Name | (PLEASE PRINT) |
| Address | Apt. # |
| City | State/Prov. | Zip/Postal Code |

Signature (if under 18, a parent or guardian must sign)

### Mail to the Harlequin® Reader Service:
**IN U.S.A.:** P.O. Box 1867, Buffalo, NY 14240-1867
**IN CANADA:** P.O. Box 609, Fort Erie, Ontario L2A 5X3

**Want to try two free books from another series?**
**Call 1-800-873-8635 or visit www.ReaderService.com.**

* Terms and prices subject to change without notice. Prices do not include applicable taxes. Sales tax applicable in N.Y. Canadian residents will be charged applicable taxes. Offer not valid in Quebec. This offer is limited to one order per household. Not valid for current subscribers to Love Inspired Historical books. All orders subject to credit approval. Credit or debit balances in a customer's account(s) may be offset by any other outstanding balance owed by or to the customer. Please allow 4 to 6 weeks for delivery. Offer available while quantities last.

**Your Privacy**—The Harlequin® Reader Service is committed to protecting your privacy. Our Privacy Policy is available online at www.ReaderService.com or upon request from the Harlequin Reader Service.

We make a portion of our mailing list available to reputable third parties that offer products we believe may interest you. If you prefer that we not exchange your name with third parties, or if you wish to clarify or modify your communication preferences, please visit us at www.ReaderService.com/consumerschoice or write to us at Harlequin Reader Service Preference Service, P.O. Box 9062, Buffalo, NY 14269. Include your complete name and address.

LIHDIR13R

# *ReaderService*.com

## Manage your account online!

- Review your order history
- Manage your payments
- Update your address

*We've designed
the Harlequin® Reader Service
website just for you.*

## Enjoy all the features!

- Reader excerpts from any series
- Respond to mailings and
  special monthly offers
- Discover new series available to you
- Browse the Bonus Bucks catalog
- Share your feedback

*Visit us at:*

# ReaderService.com